SCREAMCATCHER

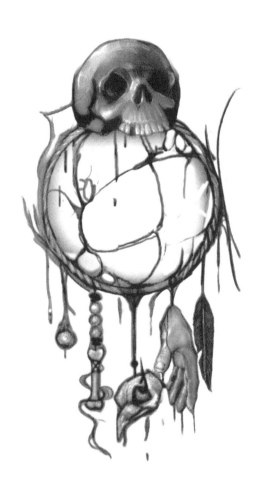

K. LAIRD AND M. WILLS

ILLUSTRATED BY EMMA MACKELA AND MIHA BRUMEC

To Luke and Cora, who never met a scary story
they didn't want to make more terrifying
and whose imaginations rekindled our own.
And, to all the kids who love to be scared – just a little.

This is a work of fiction and the characters in this book are entirely fictional. Any resemblance
to actual persons living or dead is entirely coincidental. No part of this book may be reproduced,
stored in a retrieval system, or transmitted in any form or by any means, electronic, mechanical,
photocopying, recording, or otherwise, without express written permission of the authors. For
more information, contact kelley.laird@gmail.com.

ISBN: 979-8-9898183-1-0 (hardcover) · 979-8-9898183-0-3 (paperback)
979-8-9898183-2-7 (ebook)

Illustrations by Emma Mackela and Miha Brumec
Book design by Virtual Paintbrush Book Design.

Published in Maryland, USA
First edition, September 2024

TABLE OF CONTENTS

1

In the spirit world, there is no time as we know it.
Past and future do not exist. All "time" is now.
- James Van Praagh, from *Ghosts Among Us*

THE GHOST IN THE PICTURE

He got the room ready as fast as he could. He hated being up here. How long had it been since he had last walked up the stairs? The attic was hot and musty, with pale morning light coming through the attic's one small window. Too many memories in this room. He made the bed and put her bedspread on it. His eyes caught on the design. Flowers and butterflies... He sat down, holding his head in his hands.

A cool breeze touched his skin. He looked up at the window, closed tightly. He turned and saw the painting, hanging behind the bed, still with a sheet over it. The sheet moving slightly in the breeze, making a soft whisper. He rubbed his eyes. He reached over and pulled the sheet from the painting, but he didn't look at it. He couldn't. He left the attic as quickly as he'd come, running down the stairs two at a time.

It was a cold and rainy spring afternoon when I got to my

Uncle David's farmhouse. I had flown by myself from New York City to Chicago and then rode in a car all the way to wherever I was in Indiana, all since that morning. My parents had decided to take a romantic anniversary trip in Europe, which I guess didn't involve kids, and sent me off to an uncle I had never met!

The trip had actually been pretty easy. A flight attendant walked with me through the airport, cause I'm only eight, and walked me all the way to my plane. We got hot chocolate on the way. She was chatty and talked a lot about how she loved flying, and Chicago, and other stuff. When I told her I was going to a farm in Indiana for two weeks, she smiled and laughed saying farm life was something to experience... at least once! I wasn't sure what she meant.

The plane bumped a lot in the air, which made my stomach feel sick. But I got extra snacks and two sodas because people felt sorry for me, I guess.

Another flight attendant walked me through the airport in Chicago, where we found a short friendly-looking man waiting for me at the luggage carousal. He had a picture of me with my name in large print under it- Willa Sully. "How embarrassing," I thought, while the flight attendant and the man talked.

His name was Pete. He was a friend of my dad's from a long time ago, and loved to talk. As we walked to the car and started the drive, he told me all about himself and his family. How he had wanted to be a professional baseball player growing up and played in the Minor League for 5 years before injuring his arm. He said my dad was a great baseball player too, but that he had wanted to be a lawyer so he left baseball behind. Pete came back to his hometown to take care of his parents, opened a coffee shop, got married, had two kids, but they were older, they were at summer camp. I looked out the window as Pete droned on about the town I was going to. My mom had warned me people in Indiana would seem a lot friendlier than in New York. It was kind of weird. I wondered what my few friends were doing in New York, where people hardly looked at you let alone talk to you.

We stopped at a McDonald's and Pete bought me a cheeseburger happy meal. After lunch, I must have fallen sleep. I woke up to thunder, and the sunny skies were gone, replaced with big dark storm clouds. Lightening lit up the dark sky and thunder boomed as the wipers raced back and forth across the windshield.

Seeing that I was awake, Pete started a long speech about how in Indiana, they appreciated the spring rains because farmers depended on it to water their fields, and ensure a good harvest later on. Blah blah blah.... Boy he could talk, I thought,

as I watched the flat fields and darkening skies go by. I wondered if it was raining in New York, and then I got more nervous about the next two weeks and meeting my uncle.

My parents had said little about Uncle David. I knew he was Dad's older brother. They said he was a grumpy man. He still lived on the farm where dad had grown up, working from dawn to dusk. Dad had told me staying on a real farm would be an adventure, but Mom warned me that I would need to entertain myself at the farmhouse. I was used to entertaining myself. If I was being honest, I was alone most of the time, with my parents working long hours. Sometimes I was even lonely, though that was harder for me to admit.

I asked them why Uncle David wasn't married, and all my dad said was that he used to be married, but he got divorced when I was little. I packed three books, a big puzzle, and my favorite doll, a warrior princess named Angel, who I'd had since I was barely walking.

"Do you know my uncle?" I asked, startling Pete out of his dialogue on livestock. "I've never met him. I didn't even know Dad had a brother until last week."

Pete didn't seem that surprised. "Your dad always wanted to do something important, something that would take him away from Indiana."

I asked why my dad wanted to leave Indiana so badly. Pete said that my dad's parents, my grandparents, had died in a tornado the first year my dad was at college. "After that, he didn't really have any reason to come home. Your dad and David never agreed to much. David always wanted to be a farmer, take over the family farm, and your dad, he just hated the farm life and even more after the tragedy." I was learning things I never knew. Why had Dad never told me about his

family? More lightning flashed outside, thunder rumbling seconds after.

I asked Pete if Uncle David was grumpy. "Did your dad tell you that?" Pete said, smiling. I laughed and nodded. "He's kind of gruff," Pete said, "but he's had tough times over the years. You'll get along great once you spend some time with him." I wanted to know more, but Pete said we were almost there. I looked out the window, wet with rain, and saw the same flat golden, green and black fields I had seen the entire drive. A "Welcome to Ligonier" sign passed my window. "Ligonier's a three-stoplight town," Pete said, proudly. I decided I liked Pete, though he was kind of weird. But in a good way. Kind of like I imagined that people thought of me. Quirky and a little weird.

My uncle's farm was on the outskirts of town. I felt butterflies in my tummy when we got to the farm. Pete carried my small flowery suitcase and purple backpack to the farmhouse door. The rain had lightened to a drizzle, but my brown hair was wet by the time we reached the porch, and I was cold. The farmhouse was a small white wooden shuttered home with a steeple looking roof and a small front porch. It honestly looked like a church from the road. The white paint was chipping, and the roof looked like it might leak. The porch creaked under my feet. Pete said that most farmhouses needed a new coat of paint every few years because of the storms that rolled through every spring.

"But what farmer can afford that?" he laughed. I didn't really get the joke, but I'm a city girl.

Pete knocked loudly at the door, rattling the window. No one answered. The house was dark, and the nervousness in my stomach was starting to make me nauseous. "Don't worry," Pete smiled, probably sensing my unease. "He's here somewhere, his truck is right over there. I bet he's just working in the barn." Pete put down my bags and started walking across the drive to a big red barn. It looked like red barns from books I had read, and possibly a fun place to explore. Did Uncle David have cats? Horses, even?

Before Pete had left the porch the barn door banged open, and a man walked out trailed closely by a golden retriever, big, furry, and beautiful. My jaw dropped. Bewildered, I thought for a moment Dad had traveled to this small town in Indiana, not Europe. Uncle David looked exactly like my dad! Like they could be twins! He was tall, with dark hair, and he wore of look of annoyance that I'd seen exactly before on my dad's face. As he got closer, I could see he was taller than my dad and looked a lot older with worry lines on his forehead and a streak of white down the middle of his black hair. "Like a skunk," I thought for a moment, immediately feeling guilty. Why didn't he dye his hair like my mom always did to hide her gray? I thought to myself.

David arrived at the porch and shook Pete's hand.

"Thank you, Pete," he said gruffly. He had a deep voice, like my dad. "What do I owe you in gas money for the pickup?"

"Nothing, David, seriously. Happy to help the family. And it was nice getting to know this little bird," Pete said, smiling down at me.

Uncle David turned his attention to me. "How was the trip, little miss?" he asked seriously.

I felt very shy. Uncle David loomed over me. "Good... I got to have two sodas and a happy meal on the way!"

Uncle David raised an eyebrow at Pete.

"I only got the Happy Meal for her," Pete said grinning. "Well, I better get back to town and see about the coffee shop. Nice to meet you, Willa. Come by my shop sometime, my wife and I would love to treat you to the best hot chocolate in Northern Indiana." Pete smiled, and at that, he walked to his truck and drove away.

We were left on the porch. I had no idea what to say, and I felt like Uncle David didn't know either. But the dog broke the ice. He had been sniffing my ankles during the entire conversation, and suddenly jumped up on me, giving me a big bear hug, his wet nose pressing into my cheek. He sure felt like a bear, and I knew we would be fast friends.

"Down boy," Uncle David said sternly. "This here is Ted, but he also goes by Teddy Bear. He's getting old and slow, but I guess he still has some spunk. And, he seems to like you," A small smile flashed across Uncle David's face for the first time.

I was aware of David watching me closely for several long moments as I ruffled Teddy Bear under the ears. "My goodness, you are the spitting image of my mom... and..." he trailed off and looked away. "Well, that storm doesn't seem finished quite yet, let's get inside and you can settle in." Almost in answer, thunder crackled loudly in the distance and lightening flashed through the sky brightly over the nearby fields. We quickly grabbed my stuff and went inside with Teddy Bear following close behind.

The farmhouse was dark, with little light coming through the small windows because of the storm. It smelled musty and I sneezed three times. I was allergic to dust and kicked myself for not bringing my allergy medicine.

My uncle turned on the lights, which glowed weakly, revealing the house's depressing furniture. In the living room, there was an old, sagging easy chair in front of a small table with an even smaller ancient looking TV. The kitchen had a small table with three wooden chairs in the middle of the room. The counters were clean but stained yellow and cracking. There was very little art or photos on the wall. For maybe the twentieth time today I thought of my apartment in New York, with its art, new furniture, and a new kitchen that my mom was so proud of.

There were a few old-fashioned farming landscapes and one dusty-looking framed picture of what seemed to be my dad, my uncle, and my grandparents who were all much younger, standing proudly in front of the big red barn out front with big smiles on their faces. They all looked happy together. I looked closely at my grandmother and could see what Uncle David had meant. We had the same face, slightly oval head with large brown eyes, a small narrow nose, and a big toothy smile. I guess I knew which side my genes favored. It was like looking into the future. Uncle David watched me looking at the photos, his face unreadable.

There were two bedrooms off the entryway hallway, though one looked like an office. One bathroom sat between the two. Where was I going to sleep? I didn't see any couch, and I didn't have my sleeping bag. The barn, I thought? The idea gave me shivers.

As if he had read my mind, he said "You'll be sleeping upstairs."

"Where?" I hadn't seen a staircase coming in.

"There's a back staircase in the kitchen going up to an attic bedroom," he said. He opened a door that I had thought was a pantry, showing a narrow set of wooden stairs leading up into darkness. Loud thunder crackled outside making the hairs on my arm stick up.

"I think you'll like it. It's the largest room in the house. Your dad and I shared that room as kids, and, well..." Uncle David trailed off suddenly, his face clouding.

"Anyway," he cleared his throat, "There's no bathroom up there, you'll have to share with me down here. Why don't you go upstairs and settle in and I'll start getting supper around?" Without waiting for a response, he turned to the refrigerator.

I guessed and flipped a switch outside the door, and a dim lightbulb lit the staircase. A light, cool breeze blew down the stairs, and I wondered if my uncle had left a window open. I slowly dragged my suitcase and backpack, *thunk-thunk-thunk*, up the narrow stairs. Wallpaper was peeling on both sides of the staircase. Lightning made the room upstairs briefly flash, before falling back into darkness.

I felt along the wall at the top of the stairs and flicked a switch. This room was even mustier and dustier than the downstairs had been, but it was pretty big.

Uncle David called from the doorway, "Go ahead and open that window in there. There's a latch but it should open easy enough. Sorry about the dust, I ran out of time to clean it up before you came. I'll toss you up a wet rag and you can dust a bit, if that'll help?" A wet grey towel landed at the top of the stairs.

I opened the window across the room, and a heavy, wet cold blew in, settling the dust. The fields and trees behind the house waved in the wind. A sudden bolt of lightning cut across the sky, followed quickly by loud thunder.

I turned to take in what would be my home for the next two weeks. There was a large bed with a faded pink bedspread covered with colorful butterflies and flowers. A lot bigger than my bed in New York, I thought approvingly. A small white nightstand was next to the bed with a small lamp. I picked up a music box from the nightstand and wound it. A soft lullaby played as a small metal ballerina spun slowly, paint flaking from her face and skirt. A dresser sat opposite the bed, also white and small, as if for a child. A little chair and a toy box with unicorns completed the room. Everything seemed like it was decorated for a little girl. Did my uncle decorate it just for me, I wondered? But it was so dusty... I poked through the toy box. Creepy dolls with shiny black eyes, a jack-in-the-box that I promised myself I would never wind up, some wooden animals, a metal miniature of some kind of farm equipment... I didn't think I would open that box again. The floor vibrated from thunder.

The most interesting thing in the room was the painting. It hung above the bed, and no matter where I went in the room, I always found my eyes drawn to it, like a magnet. It showed a lovely fall scene. A white farmhouse occupied the left foreground; a lot like this one. Trees with red and yellow leaves in the yard, a field of yellow corn and white flowers stretched out to the right and behind the farmhouse. A colorful line of trees in the distance marked the end of the field. The painting was beautiful and ordinary, but what captured my attention was the strange... shape... in the field. Was it a person? I couldn't tell. The flowers and corn seemed to bend around the whitish form as if it moved steadily through the field. I decided that the painting creeped me out. And it was hanging directly above where I'd sleep!

After I wiped down the room and unpacked my things, I

came downstairs to the kitchen. At the table, spaghetti and tomato sauce with peas and a large glass of milk were waiting.

"Thank you," I said, sitting down at the table, "I'm starving."

"Make sure you wash your hands before you eat," my uncle said. I went to the sink to wash my hands, and then after drying them on the towel on the refrigerator, I sat down to eat.

After that, Uncle David brought his own plate to the table. Teddy Bear walked in from the living room and laid down under the table with his head on my feet.

While we ate, we talked about my life in New York, and I finally started feeling relaxed after my long day. Uncle David asked me about my parents and their work.

"They're lawyers," I said. "They work alllllll the time!"

"Are they happy?"

I was quiet for a few moments. "I guess. I don't know. The question should be, am I happy?" I tried to spin the spaghetti on to my fork, the way Mom had shown me.

Uncle David watched me in that unreadable way of his and changed the subject. "Does your dad ever talk about Indiana? Has he talked about me?" It seemed like he had been waiting to ask this question.

I didn't know what to say. "Not really... I don't remember." He went quiet and we finished eating in silence.

At the end of the meal, I asked to be excused. My mind turned to the narrow staircase, and the large creepy room, and the painting. "By the way, thanks for the room. It's perfect. But, um, did you decorate it for me?"

My uncle looked away suddenly. "Honestly, no. That's just how it's been for the last decade." He got up, grabbed both of our plates, and headed to the sink.

"The painting above the bed... Is it this farmhouse? Who painted it?" I was curious.

He stopped washing dishes and looked out the kitchen window. He took a long time to answer. "Yeah, it's a nice painting, isn't it? Yeah, it's this farmhouse in the fall, right before Halloween."

I thought about the shape in the field. The way it seemed to move, while the rest of the painting was still... "What's the th-...." I started.

He turned to me, interrupting. "Willa, your parents told me you need to read or do a puzzle in the evenings, and that you should only watch a half hour of TV a day. I also like to read in the evenings. I've got some work to do in the office for a bit, but after that, let's have a reading hour in the living room. Does that sound good?" He nodded once and left the kitchen.

"Okay," I said quietly.

Before long I could feel the long day weighing on me. I was exhausted. I went to the small bathroom, brushed my teeth, washed my face, and came back to the living room. Teddy Bear trailed me through the house. I said goodnight and headed for the stairs, Teddy Bear on my heels. David's eyes peeked over his newspaper. "Remember to keep the window open. It gets pretty stuffy upstairs." His eyes and then his forehead quickly disappeared again behind the paper. "Sleep tight." I gave Teddy Bear a hug at the foot of the stairs, and said goodnight to him again. Teddy Bear laid down and watched me ascend, bright black eyes following my every step.

The window was still open from earlier, and the air was crisp and cool. The storm was gone, and the moonlit field behind the house was bright and still. I looked out in the field, and for a brief moment wondered if I would see a nameless shape moving steadily through the corn. But the field was peaceful, almost idyllic, and I climbed into bed. I read for only a few minutes before falling asleep, the bedside lamp still on.

A sudden sound startled me awake. Disoriented in the dark, I reached instinctively for my reading lamp overhead, but nothing... where was it? I looked around, confused, and a few seconds passed until I remembered I was in Indiana, not New York. Teddy Bear barked again outside. Why was my lamp off? I reached blindly for the nightstand and bumped the music box, which let out a few sad, slow musical notes. I turned on the lamp and found my watch. 1 AM. I had to pee. I hated the idea of going down the narrow staircase to the bathroom and its cold tile floor below.

My heartbeat started to return to normal. Ted's barking had startled me. I wondered what had startled him. My mom always told me to listen to the sounds at night and name them, one by one, to get over my fear of the dark. So, I kept listening. The crickets were chirping, frogs were croaking. The wind whistled. An owl hooted. The field rustled. The house creaked. All sounds I knew, nothing to be scared about, I told myself.

After a few long minutes had passed, I went downstairs to pee. The house seemed larger and emptier at night. The whistling of the wind upstairs became a low moaning on the ground floor. The shadows in the corners of the living room were a thick, inky black. I could feel my imagination wanting to see something in those shadows, something watching me, waiting. I kept my eyes on the ground and hurried to the bathroom. On my way back to bed, my heart almost stopped when another, louder sound cut through the soft moan and creak of the old house. I shivered with relief when I recognized the whimpering of Teddy Bear at the back door. I let him in, and he followed me upstairs and jumped into the bed, rolling on his back to beg for a belly rub. I felt the tension flowing out of my body.

And yet... I looked around the room. Something was different. I felt it in my gut, but what was it? The lamp was on, the music box next to it. The big bed, toy box, dresser, her luggage, the painting... everything was the same. I climbed into bed uncertainly, absentmindedly rubbing Teddy's belly, and leaned over to turn off the bedside lamp.

I froze, my eyes on the painting above me. My sense of unease that something was different came back, stronger. I came to my knees and looked closely at the painting, my nose inches above its surface. The shape was closer. I was sure of it. It was emerging from the field behind the farmhouse, its form clearly now the size of a child. It did look like a child, I thought. A child wearing a white sheet or blanket or something. Two dark dots were barely visible where the face would have been. They were eye cutouts, I realized, like a cheap ghost costume. Stretching behind it through the field was the clear path it had carved, walking slowly through the corn. It was facing directly toward me. I exhaled shakily, realizing I had been holding my breath, but I had a horrible moment of panic when I thought I felt a soft cool breeze tickle my face.

I'm just being stupid, I thought? The window is open. Paintings don't change. It looked like that before. I could be dreaming right now. I fell back on my pillow and willed myself to keep my eyes on Teddy Bear. It took a long time for me to fall back asleep, the lamp still on.

The morning came with bright sunlight streaming through the open window, birds chirping and the smell of bacon in the air. The night's events were distant and half-forgotten. Teddy Bear had left during the night. I was starving and got dressed quickly. I took a step onto the staircase, hesitated, and looked back at the painting.

The ghost was larger. It was closer the farmhouse. I turned away, suddenly queasy, and I rushed downstairs.

David was in a hurry. "Morning. Eat quick, we need to head to town and run a few errands. I've got a long day in the field ahead, so you'll have plenty of time to explore and relax later." He was pulling on his boots already. "You slept later than I thought you would."

"Sorry for that, I guess I was more tired from everything yesterday than I thought." I was thinking of a way to ask about the painting again when he set out eggs and bacon in front of me.

"Eat up, we leave in ten minutes," and he walked out the back door and to the barn.

Soon, we were in his truck on the way to Ligonier. The grocery store was already busy, which David called the "farmer crowd", coming to get what they needed before a day on the farm. Everyone was really friendly, and I found myself enjoying saying hello to everyone I passed. David said hi to everyone, but he was on a mission, completing his list quickly and avoiding getting drawn into conversation. I thought he seemed moody, but didn't say anything.

Back in the truck, I asked, "Uncle David, is it okay if we stop by Pete's coffee shop for a hot chocolate before heading back to the house? He said had just the best hot chocolate in Indiana, if I came by..." I trailed off.

That familiar look of annoyance flashed across his face, but he nodded. "I have to go by the post office, so I'll drop you off at Pete's and be back to grab you when I'm done. Sound good?"

"Yes! Thank you, Uncle David!" I loved hot chocolate and couldn't wait to try the "best." David glanced at me and smiled.

The coffee shop was small, narrow, and cluttered, but had a warm homey feeling. It felt really different from the Starbucks I usually went to in New York, which felt sterile and full of people racing to get to their next destination. I liked it a lot. White tables and chairs and fake sunflowers and pots were in each of the two windows. The walls were decorated with family photos going back generations, with many in black and white.

I didn't see Pete at first and felt a little nervous. I realized I had forgot to ask my uncle for money. Two older men sitting by the window turned to watch me enter. As I made my way to the counter, Pete came out from a back room and smiled. I smiled back and waved.

"Well, hi there, little traveler! How was your first night on the farm?" Pete said warmly.

"It was good. I love Teddy Bear!" I said in return. A slender woman with her greying hair pulled into a ponytail emerged from the back room and walked over to Pete, a questioning look in her eyes.

"This is my wife, Joey," Pete said. "Joey, this is Brian's girl, Willa, visiting from New York. She's staying with David for the next two weeks."

"Please to meet you Willa." Joey walked around the counter and bent down. Her eyes sparkled with her smile. "How are you liking it on the farm?"

"The farm's pretty!" I said honestly. "I'm going to explore around more today. Especially the barn."

"I think you'll find there's a lot to discover. It might seem a little boring to someone from a big city, but it's peaceful and beautiful." Joey said seriously.

Pete rolled his eyes at Joey. "How about that hot chocolate, little miss?" He grinned at my vigorous nod, and began to make a cup. Joey stood up. "Come and visit us any time, Willa. If you need a break from the farm, we'd love to show you around time, go to some playgrounds, whatever you like." She returned behind the counter, turning her attention to a new customer.

Pete was humming softly to himself while he made my hot chocolate. Before I knew what I was doing, I said, "Does Uncle David paint?"

He raised an eyebrow as he handed me a steaming cup. "That's a strange question! Now, be careful, that's fresh and hot."

I told him about the painting in my attic room of the farmhouse. I mentioned that I thought there was a kid wearing some kind of ghost costume in the picture, but I didn't say anything about it moving when I wasn't looking. In the coffee shop, drinking hot chocolate on a sunny morning, it seemed too ridiculous to mention.

Pete looked thoughtfully, "Becky used to paint a bit, I think. Becky, that was David's wife. Probably one of her pieces, I'd guess."

"Who's the ghost in the picture?" I asked.

"Well... If it was Becky, I'd guess that..." But Pete trailed off as David walked in. He, Pete, and Joey talked for a few minutes while I tried to think of a way to get Pete's attention. I had to know what Pete had been about to say.

But David turned to look at me. "Sorry Willa, but we need to head back. Morning's getting away from me, and I've got a lot to do." Pete quickly put my hot chocolate in a to-go cup.

"How's the hot chocolate? Haven't had better, have you?" he asked playfully. I hadn't, and told him so. He smiled and squeezed my shoulder before turning back to the counter. Uncle David and I headed back to the truck.

Back at the farmhouse, Uncle David hopped out of the truck and went to the barn. I asked if I could explore around the barn too.

"Sure," he said, "But please stay out of the way of any heavy equipment. I'm going to get the tractor and plow the back field before lunchtime. Feel free to poke around in the barn, you might even find some old toys up in the loft. Keep your eye out for Missy and her friends," he added, winking. "There are also lots of hay bales to jump around on. But again, I'd feel badly if you hurt yourself on my watch, so don't get crazy."

I spent the morning playing in the barn. I couldn't find any toys, but the barn did have cats after all! Missy, the mom, and Missy's kittens! I had a blast jumping from hay bale to hay bale, playing the hot lava game and trying not to step on the wooden floorboards. I discovered that hours had passed when the tractor started making its way back from the fields behind the house. I had just found a knotted rope that I could swing on if I climbed up a few steps on the ladder to the hay loft. I couldn't wait to try it, but for now I went outside and waited for my uncle. I was hungry for lunch.

"Hi!" I said to Uncle David when he got off the tractor followed by Teddy Bear. "The barn is so fun. You have so many cats! Where's the dad cat? I am so hungry. How was, uh, the farming?" I tried but couldn't remember anything Pete had told me about farming.

Uncle David looked amused. "It was a fine morning. I got a lot done. You're hungry?"

"Actually, I'm starving," I said, scratching Teddy Bear around the ears.

"Grilled cheese sound good? Let's get inside and you can help me make it. I picked up some chips and baby carrots too." Uncle David smiled at me as we walked to the house. I shared with him all the fun things I'd been doing as we went inside with Teddy Bear at our heels.

"Why don't you wash up for lunch?" Uncle David suggested kindly. I was filthy, I realized, looking down at my hay-covered and dusty clothes. "I have to check something on my computer, and then we'll make our sandwiches." He headed toward his office.

"Sure." I went to the bathroom and began washing my face and hands. I couldn't believe how dirty I was! I had only been in the barn for a few hours. I laughed at the dirty sweat streaks down my cheeks and the grime that came off when I washed my hands.

I decided to change my clothes. I ran up the narrow staircase and got changed, eager to return to the barn. The next two weeks were looking better than they had since I first found out my parents were going on a trip to Europe. Playing with Teddy Bear and the kittens and visiting Pete and Joey was going to be epic! I turned to the stairs, my mind bursting with fun ideas.

A cool breeze blew against my neck, chilling me, followed by a low murmuring sound. I turned, curious. My eyes took in the closed window, and then the painting. I felt my breath go out of me. Goosebumps rose on my arms. The ghost child was close, much closer than this morning. It had crossed most of the yard, past the apple tree and the old well. The eye holes were pitch black, sagging on the face of whoever or whatever was underneath the sheet. It was raising one of its arms, outstretched toward me. The large white sheet covered whatever grasping hand or claw lay underneath! I felt I could almost see it move ever so slightly closer as I watched, the sheet rippling with its movement, and if I stayed longer the ghost would soon touch the surface of the painting, would press through the surface...

"That... can't... it's not possible!" I said out loud to no one, and I felt sick to my stomach. My excitement for the day from seconds ago had evaporated. I walked to the bed, climbed on top, and tried to pull the painting off the wall. I wanted to show it to my uncle, to get it away from my room. It wouldn't budge from the wall. I heard a low growl behind me and turned to see Teddy Bear come up the stairs, growling at me.

"Whoa boy, it's okay," I said, shakily. I had never seen any sign of aggression from Teddy before. He jumped on to the bed, and when I tried again to pull the painting from the wall he nipped and tugged at my clothes while continuing his low growl. "Ouch, Teddy stop it!" I hopped off the bed and ran downstairs, with the dog close at my heels.

Uncle David was in the kitchen getting out bread and

cheese for our sandwiches. He looked up at me in surprise as I raced into the room. Breathlessly, I said, "There is a ghost in the painting upstairs. In my room. The ghost is moving in the painting... since I got here yesterday, and it is just getting bigger and bigger and bigger. What is happening?"

Uncle David watched me. He very still. He swallowed. "I don't know what you've seen in that painting, but stuff in paintings don't move. That's not possible. Maybe you're tired from all that barn play and travel. We can cover up that painting with a sheet tonight, would that make you feel better?" he asked.

"I saw the ghost move in that painting," I said stubbornly. Why wouldn't he take me seriously? "What is that painting? Where did it come from?"

Uncle David grew quiet. He looked away, out the kitchen window. "Becky." He said softly.

"Who's Becky?"

"Becky was my wife. She was a painter. We divorced five years ago. Too much water under the bridge, so to speak. It just got too tough to stay together." He sighed deeply. He looked so tired. Teddy Bear nuzzled his hand.

"So, who's that ghost in the picture?" I asked again.

He shook his head. "Look, I don't have time for this now, I've got to get back to the field. The afternoon is slipping away." He started to walk to the door, leaving the unmade sandwiches behind on the counter.

"No!" I was determined to not avoid this conversation again. "Tell me! Why won't you tell me? I am not going back in that room if you don't tell me the truth."

Uncle David collapsed into a chair. He rubbed a hand over his face. "Willa... the person in that painting is your cousin. My daughter. Kayla."

"You have a daughter?" I was so confused. Why had I never known about my Uncle David? About my cousin Kayla?

"I had a daughter. She died ten years ago, when she was your age."

"I'm so sorry!" I sat down next to him, my anger vanished. "I had no idea. I'm sorry. How... how did she die?" I immediately regretted the question. He looked so sad.

"It's okay. It's been ten years. Even though she's been gone longer than she was with us, I still miss her every day. You remind me of her, you know. You would have been friends. She loved to read and do puzzles and get up to no good in the barn. You two are two peas in a pod." He sighed deeply. "She drowned. We were out for a picnic and a swim. Becky and I were arguing, who knows what about, and we were distracted. She drowned." His voice choked up with a sob.

"She was a great swimmer. She never got tired in the water. At the lake she'd swim back and forth from the dock to the raft all day if we'd let her. I don't know, maybe she got a cramp. Anyway, that's what the coroner said." His eyes were wet and red.

"After that, Becky and I, well, we never forgave ourselves or each other. We stayed together for a while after, but that was really when it ended. She spent lots of time upstairs painting in Kayla's room. That particular painting, well, Kayla loved Halloween. She loved the fall, with the changing colors and the golden fields and Halloween. Becky, I think wanted to capture that."

He smiled softly. "Becky and I never got over losing her. We split up after a couple years, got divorced three years after that." Uncle David looked down at his hands.

I realized I was crying too. I came around the table and hugged him. "I'm sorry. She sounds wonderful." I finally got it. Why the room was decorated as it was, why Pete had said that Uncle David had experienced a lot of tragedy. I couldn't imagine losing someone in my family. Uncle David smiled at me and hugged me back.

Later that evening, my uncle gave me a sheet to put over the painting. "Just don't look at it, and it shouldn't bother you. You have a good night sleep, and tomorrow, I'll show you how to use the rope swing the barn. That was Kayla's favorite thing to do, swing from the ladder into the hay piles. You should also come riding around on the tractor with me, she loved that." He came over and gave me a warm hug.

"It's great having you here. I know I'm not the easiest person to get along with, but I sure am enjoying the company. And I'm glad you can see where your family comes from." He kissed me on the top of my head, just like my dad did.

"Thanks Uncle David. The last couple days have been great, I can't wait to explore the farm more," I said truthfully. I did enjoy the farm a lot more than I had expected, and I wondered if I would come back to visit again with my parents in the future. He smiled and went back to his room.

My thoughts turned to the attic bedroom and the painting, and my stomach turned. I had avoided the room since lunch. My uncle either didn't know or didn't want to believe that the painting was haunted. Knowing that my cousin Kayla was the ghost in the picture didn't make me any less nervous. What did she want? Was she trying to communicate? Was she angry that some strange girl was in her bed? Was she imprisoned in the painting somehow and hoped to drag me in with her?

By the time I had gotten to the top of the stairs, I had decided I wouldn't look at the painting. If I didn't see it, it couldn't scare me, right? So, I felt my way across the room in the dark, making my way to the bed. Once on the bed, I felt my way to the picture, and I threw the sheet over it. I immediately felt much better.

I took out my book and flipped on the bedside lamp to read. I fell asleep quickly with the soft glow of the lamp.

I slept restlessly. In my dreams, the ghost pursued me. I moved through the farmhouse, my heart in my throat, and the black empty eyes of the ghost watched me, arm outstretched, through mirrors, reflected in windows, looming in shadows. In the dream the ghost was soaking wet, the sheet clinging to the body underneath, an icy bluish hand thrust toward me. I had to get away, I had to flee that blank gaze. I woke suddenly, with a cold sweat on my brow. My eyes open, I looked up at the sheet still draped over the painting, and a mad curiosity inside me demanded that I look at the painting. I had to prove that my fears were ridiculous, that painting didn't move. I sat up, my heart racing, and my courage left me as quickly as it had come, and I left the sheet where it was.

Like the night before, I had to pee, and I lay listening to the night sounds. Be like a scientist, I thought... that is the sound of a frog, there's the sound of the house's old pipes, that's just wind rattling a downstairs window. A scratching sound eluded my deduction, until I remembered the previous night. That must be the dog, I thought. Does he usually sleep outside? If he does, why has he been scratching to come in? As if to confirm my thinking, I heard a small whine at the kitchen door downstairs.

I decided to get up, grabbing a flashlight Uncle David had lent to me. I opened the back door to find a very happy and energetic Teddy Bear. He stood on his hind legs to lick my face. "Good boy," I said, but he was already racing past me, running up the stairs to my room with a small bark. "Where are you going so fast?" I whispered up at him. He must be excited to cuddle up again tonight, I thought, and I was comforted to think he'd be in my bed when I got back from the bathroom.

Dim, early morning light was started to shine in my window as I made my way back to bed. I shined my flashlight on the bed to find Teddy sitting at attention facing me, his tongue lolling out of his mouth as he panted happily. I flicked off the light and climbed into bed. As I pulled up my bedsheet, I felt something unfamiliar. Another blanket? I thought with confusion. I pulled it closer, looking at it. A white sheet.

I gasped in horror and looked up. The sheet had fallen from the painting. My unsettling dream came back to me in a rush. In the room's faint light, I looked at the painting, dreading what I would see.

The ghost was nowhere to be seen. The painting was a peaceful scene of the farm in autumn, with no trace of the ghost that had haunted me for the past few days. Had I imagined it somehow? I wondered. The floor creaked. I turned.

The ghost stood at the foot of my bed. The white sheet hung over it, black eye cutouts watching me, its head tilted to one side in curiosity. I felt a scream in my throat, but it wouldn't come out. It raised its arms slowly. I pushed my back against the wall, clenching my pillows!

The ghost pulled off the sheet, revealing a brown-haired smiling young girl. She said, "Hi, my name is Kayla. Do you want to play?"

I fainted. When I woke later, the sun was shining fully

through the window. Teddy was licking my face, and Kayla was sitting cross legged next to me, waiting patiently.

For the rest of my time in Indiana, Kayla was my constant friend. Uncle David never asked, but he must have wondered how I knew where the old tree swing was, where to find the fishing poles, and about the pond beyond the corn field. He knew I was having too much fun in the corn field and the barn. And I was. Playing hide and seek, ghost in the graveyard, and all sorts of other games that Kayla knew. I loved Indiana, and I loved my uncle and Kayla, my ghostly cousin who played on the farm with me during the day, and returned to the farm in the painting every night.

2

"The monsters that rose from the dead,
they are nothing compared to the ones
we carry in our hearts."
-Max Brooks, *World War Z:
An Oral History of the Zombie War*

THE NIGHT CRAWLERS

I woke with a start. My heart throbbed in my chest, blood pulsing loudly in my ears. A sound? Had I heard something? I lay there, heart pounding in the dark, waiting for it to come again for what seemed like an hour. "A nightmare," I whispered to myself, breathing deeply.

I closed my eyes and it came again. "What was that?" I thought, and I sat up in bed, reaching for my flashlight on the nightstand. A cracking, scratching, shuffling sound, loud but distant. The sound was outside. An animal in the bushes? Not a deer or fox, it was making too much noise. I almost called out to my mom and dad, but remembered they were both working late at the factory and going to a work party after their shift.

I got out of bed. Knowing my parents were out, the silence of the house suddenly felt cavernous. I walked slowly to the window and drew aside the curtains, carefully in case someone was trying to get into the house. The yard was empty. It was a moonless night, but the streetlamp by the corn field across the street dimly lit the yard. With no moon, no wind, and no cars on the road the yard seemed unreal, a picture from a scary book.

After a few moments my eyes caught on something. The walkway running to the street seemed... soiled in some way, like my dad had been out gardening all day and forgotten to sweep. My hand tightened on my flashlight, and in a moment of recklessness I turned it on and illuminated the walk. I regretted it at once! The yellow, shaking beam of the flashlight fell on footprints, dark, shining wetly. They approached the front door. I leaned forward as far as I could with the flashlight and saw the glistening prints on the lowest steps of the front porch. I looked at them, spellbound, my breath caught in my throat. They looked reddish, smeared in places. Blood, I thought. It looks just like blood.

A crashing sound of breaking glass came from downstairs, shattering the quiet and shocking me to my senses. I whirled around, the flashlight on the door. I could hear a guttural grunting noise... a bear? I thought wildly. Maybe the Davisons' dog got rabies?

A heavy footstep fell on the staircase. Another. Then another, the stair creaking loudly, and I knew the thing was coming up the stairs. My room was the only room at the top of the stairs. I was paralyzed with fear.

The snuffling groaning sound grew louder. Was this a nightmare? I looked down at myself, wondering if I should pinch myself or if I could will myself awake. I closed my eyes, counting my breaths. Surely, I would wake any second...

Another heavy footstep, and I knew it was on the other side of the door. Ragged breathing, and then the doorknob rattled as something grabbed hold of it. My eyes flew open, I could

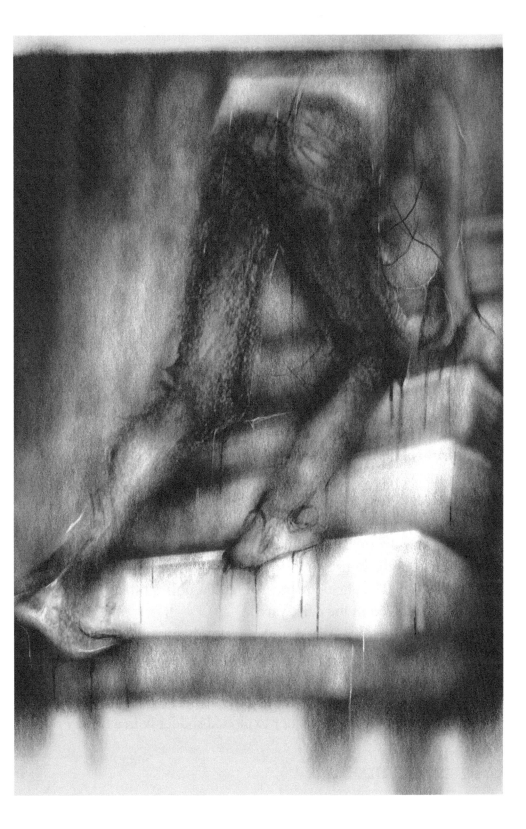

finally move again, and I raced across the room, locking the door just as the knob began to turn. I backed away, watching the knob turn, and turn again, as the thing tried to open the door. The door began to shudder under blows from the heavy fists or paws or claws of whatever thing was on the other side. The wooden doorframe shook and began to splinter. I could hear the door beginning to crack with each strike.

I ran to the window and pulled it open. A small ledge ran under the window and around to the roof on either side. I stepped one leg through and looked back. Another pounding strike and the center of the door cracked wide, wooden shards spraying across my carpet. A hand, blackened and discolored and covered in sores, reached through, pulling the wood of the door apart. A deep growl came from the other side, the thing sensing how close it was to me. I climbed out of the window and scurried on to the narrow roof, making my way toward the chimney, trying to get as far away from that thing as possible. From my room, I could hear the door explode in ruins and the thing roared in satisfaction as it entered my room.

Headlights were coming down the lane, toward the farmhouse. "Mom!" I screamed, feeling such a wave of relief that I was dizzy. They would know what to do. The car pulled in front of the house and I saw it wasn't my parents' car but a police car. The car door opened, and a police officer stepped out, shadowed in the dark yard.

"Help me!" I cried out. I saw her startle. "There's something in the house!" The police officer approached the house warily, one hand holding her baton and the other on her weapon.

The corn field behind her exploded suddenly in a frenzy of

running, shambling forms. Lit only by the pale streetlamp, the creatures, the *zombies*, rushed out of the corn, mouths gaping open, rotting arms reaching forward. The police officer, hearing their movement, began to turn. Too slowly. "Look! Behind you!" I shrieked helplessly. The zombies were too close.

I shut my eyes and covered my ears. Tears covered my cheeks. I felt the cold chimney next to me, pressing gently against my face. It can't be real, I whispered to myself. I can't...

And my mom gently whispered in my ear, "Wake up honey, you're having a bad dream." I could feel her holding a cold washcloth to my cheek. I shuddered as a wave of calm passed through me.

I opened my eyes and looked at her. The face looking back at me was blackened and rotten, her eyes milky-white. I screamed and screamed!

"Honey, don't freak out! We had a Halloween party at work! This is my costume!" My mom laughed, removing her mask.

I didn't sleep for the rest of the night.

3

"We think we are done with the pandemic,
but the pandemic is not done with us."
-Gitanjali Pai, MD

QUARANTINE

It was the middle of the night when we arrived at the hotel. The street was deserted, with one dim streetlamp illuminating the hotel's entrance. The old white façade of the hotel loomed over the street, and a faded sign identified the building as the Whitehall Palace. Large white pillars and dusty oval windows framed the entrance, hinting at a more palatial past. Our van pulled in front of the entrance, and two men in yellow hazmat suits approached the vehicle.

"I don't want to stay here, Dad." My daughter Charlotte looked out the window at the hotel with growing alarm. "I know, honey. Me neither," I said, wearily. "We'll just have to make the best of it. I'm sure time will fly by." The men opened the van doors.

I feel like we're being treated like criminals," I muttered to my wife, Tracy, as we stepped out of the van. "I know. Me too," she said, sadly. We were returning home from five years overseas. My daughter had been born abroad, and this was her first experience in America. America during the pandemic. Charlotte would probably need some therapy after this experience, I thought. Lock downs, masks, plastic face shields, full body suits. No kindergarten. Everyone so afraid of being around other people. So many deaths. It had been a nightmare overseas, and it didn't look like it was going to be much better back home. Hopefully vaccines would soon put the worst of the pandemic in the rearview mirror.

For now, though, we were facing two weeks of quarantine at this ancient hotel. We had discovered this fact when we had checked in for our flight from Thailand, twenty hours ago. This was new information, but the entire year had been full of changing plans. We could handle this one last hurdle. With negative tests in hand, we had boarded the plane, crossed the Pacific in masks and face shields, and were now being dropped off in the middle of the night by an unfriendly van driver with a plastic barricade between the driver's seat and our back section at a random hotel in Chicago's Southside.

The two men in hazmat suits shambled up to the van. On closer inspection, the suits looked more like protection gear for scuba divers from another era, and were they wearing 1930s gas masks? They grabbed our luggage and grunted for us to follow them.

The Whitehall Palace looked like it was falling apart. Its windows were mostly dark, its parking lot empty. It was hard to tell in the dark, but I didn't have a good feeling about it.

The front desk clerk greeted us at the door. His grey eyes crinkled over his mask, apparently indicating a smile. Like everything else with this place, the clerk had seen better days. His uniform was aged and wrinkled, his short hair disheveled. We put our luggage on a cart, and the clerk pushed it into a side entrance. I looked back as the van pulled away quickly, sped around the corner, and was gone.

"Please leave the luggage here. We'll spray it down to sanitize it and have it up to your rooms in no time." He gave his maybe-smile again. It was hard to tell. "Sorry about all the safety procedures. Believe it or not, things are getting better, but there are still a lot of rules for international travelers. Please follow me," and he led them into the hotel lobby.

The lobby was large and completely empty. A small crystal chandelier hung in the center. Empty flower vases adorned tables along the walls. Charlotte and my son Will collapsed into a shapeless yellow couch as they waited for me to check in, sending up a small cloud of dust. The clerk circled around the front desk. A blank television hung on the wall behind him. The computer screen bathed the clerk's face in ghostly white light as he checked us in.

"Per procedure, we'll bring meals to your rooms three times a day. We'll ring the bell beforehand, please wear a mask when we arrive. We'll do your laundry once a week and clean your rooms once every four days. During the cleaning, you'll be asked to wear your masks and face shields and go into the adjoining room and then the other while cleaning is underway. You are not allowed to leave your rooms at any time during the next two weeks. If you leave your rooms, you'll be placed under further quarantine procedures and the local health authorities will be notified." His voice was a flat monotone.

"You can always reach me by dialing 0, and I'll be as responsive as I can. As you may have noticed, we don't have guests. We're running on a skeleton staff, there's only a few of us to run the front desk, the kitchen, and the laundry. The government designated us a quarantine hotel over a year ago, but we haven't had that any quarantine travelers recently. Right now, you're it."

We shambled behind him to our rooms. Ornate gold leaf décor and faded tapestries lined the wall. We passed unlit hallways that stretched to other parts of the hotel. The hotel was just conserving energy, I thought, though it felt like we were walking into crypt. We passed through a doorway that was cordoned with yellow tape, like a crime scene. A paper sign taped to the door read QUARANTINE WING - NO ENTRANCE. "I don't like this," Tracy whispered to me as we walked.

I felt like a terrible father and husband, then. I had been trying to put on a brave face for the last 24 hours, but now I wasn't sure this trip was worth this draconian treatment. It felt like we were being put in jail, and while I understood some of the health implications, it still felt harsh.

Our adjoining rooms were simple but clean, thankfully. The bathrooms smelled of mildew. Windows faced an indoor courtyard, looking down on an empty pool. Windows from other rooms lined the courtyard, all black and vacant. I closed the curtains quickly.

"I'll bring your luggage in no time," the clerk repeated. "Call me if you need anything." He shut the door. I couldn't believe that we were supposed to spend two weeks in these rooms. How would we pass the time? It was a problem for tomorrow, I thought. Will and Charlotte were already asleep in the other room.

I woke with a gasp in the dark room. One of the kids had called out to me in the dark. I walked into the adjoining room, where Will was sitting up in bed, his eyes wide with fright. "The closet light turned on. Just a minute ago." I turned and saw the outline of the closet door, illuminated by its interior light. I walked over and opened the door. Empty. The light turned off when I shut the door.

"Probably just a glitch or something. It's an old hotel. No big deal," I said, as much to myself as to Will. "Let's try to get some sleep." As I walked back into my room, I began to faintly hear a baby crying somewhere in the hotel. It sounded far away.

"Do you hear that?" My wife said from the bed. Her eyes were wide, shining in the dark. "Didn't the guy say we were alone in the hotel?"

"Maybe another family arrived after us?" I walked to the front door and opened it, leaning out into the hallway. The baby's cries echoed from far down the long, empty hall. There was no other sound. I looked at my watch. 5 AM. Close enough, I thought. I went and took a long shower.

When I came out of the bathroom the baby had stopped crying. The rest of the family was awake, sitting in bed with Tracy. Jet lag, I thought. With no windows facing outside, time felt meaningless. "Who needs breakfast and coffee?"

The food was delivered at 7 AM, just as the clerk had said. We opened the door and there it was: a cart with two large silver trays with silver lids. We wheeled it in the room eagerly. The food was disgusting. Worse than the plane food. Hard bread rolls, mushy scrambled eggs, watery orange juice, no silverware. "No wonder this place doesn't have any guests," Tracy said.

I called the front desk. The same clerk from the night before answered. "Sorry sir. The head chef left a few weeks ago." He did not sound very apologetic, I thought. When did he sleep? "We really are running on a skeleton staff. We'll try to make it better." This was going to be a long two weeks.

The day passed slowly. We were groggy from jet lag and lazed in bed, watching dumb TV and playing simple games on our phones. The hotel didn't have WiFi and I couldn't get a phone connection. I felt cranky and claustrophobic. I called the front desk and let it ring at least twenty times before hanging up.

I woke from a nap that afternoon to find Charlotte standing by the windows, her face pressed to the glass. "Charlotte... what...?"

"There are people looking at us." Her tone was flat.

I rubbed my face, trying to wake myself up. "What do you mean?"

"In the windows. There are people over there, watching us."

I got out of bed and joined her. Across the big ornate internal hotel courtyard with a large empty swimming pool in the center, the many black hotel windows glared back, like the shiny eyes of some enormous spider creature. I didn't see anyone.

"Just wait a second, you'll see them. They were there a minute ago." She walked into the adjoining room. I stood for a few more moments, looking across the courtyard anxiously. I did feel like I was being watched. I should ask the clerk to close the curtains in the other rooms, I thought. I drew the curtains shut.

A chill passed through me, starting from the base of my neck and tracing down to my feet. The hair on the back of my neck stood straight up. It may have been weirdest sensation I'd ever felt. I don't believe in ghosts. Growing up, my family loved the macabre and spooky, and we went to our fair share of haunted houses, hoping to see ghosts for real. But, after many years and a lot of fake news, I had written off the idea of a spirit world. Alive and dead were two sides of a coin. Yet, at that moment, it almost felt like a ghost had come up behind and breathed on my neck.

Will and Tracy were trying again to access the internet, poking their screens angrily. "Dad, I am going to literally go crazy if we have no internet for two weeks," Will said. I had to admit that I agreed.

I shook off my unease, and I called the front desk. The clerk answered, his voice sounding distant and distracted. "I apologize sir. We have been having problems with our wireless."

"You can't expect a family with two young kids to entertain themselves in a hotel room for two weeks with no internet."

"Indeed not, sir. I will see what I can do." The clerk replied calmly.

"Also, can we order food from outside the hotel? Do you have any pizza places or restaurants nearby you'd suggest?" I couldn't imagine what the hotel would provide for dinner. I did not want to find out.

"The rooms you are in cannot call outside phone lines. Earlier during the pandemic, we had some problems with quarantined guests trying to get out before their two weeks was up. The authorities advised us to limit their communications."

I rubbed my eyes. Worse and worse, I thought. "That seems pretty severe." Tracy looked up from her book, raising her eyebrows.

"I agree," the clerk said. "Will there be anything else?"

I hung up. Dinner was a greasy but edible pizza. As we watched a movie, the sound of a crying baby began again. It sounded close, much closer than before. I muted the television. "Is that a baby?" Charlotte asked.

"There's another family quarantining in the hotel," I replied as I walked quickly to the door. As I leaned out into the hallway, the crying stopped as abruptly as it had started. Most of the lights in the hallway were off. I walked to the nearest couple rooms and leaned my ear to the door. Nothing. I swallowed, calming myself before reentering our room. The last thing we needed was the kids starting to freak out.

"The baby must have gone back to sleep," I said, trying to sound confident as I returned. The kids watched me with unease in their eyes.

At about midnight I awoke to find all the lights on in our room. Disoriented, I staggered out of bed to check on the kids. Their room was also fully lit, and both Will and Charlotte were stirring awake.

"Tracy. Tracy, wake up." I shook her shoulder gently. "Did you turn on the lights?"

She woke, annoyed and then alarmed. "What? No, of course not..." The kids walked in, looking scared.

A heavy thud shook the wall next to our bed, hard enough to rattle the light fixture. We all jumped in shock. Charlotte screamed. It repeated, and again, and again, becoming a steady pounding as if furniture was being slammed against the wall in the next room.

The lights flared brighter for a moment and then went out. The pounding ceased.

"My God, what is going on..." I murmured. Will was clutching my side, petrified. Tracy stood from the bed, staring at me in astonishment. Where was Charlotte? I whirled around and saw her standing by the window, her face pale. "Dad... look..."

I looked. The previously black windows across the ornate internal courtyard were filled with pale faces. Ghostly faces, framed by the windows, silently watching us, expressionless. Men, women, and children. A soft red light pulsed in the rooms behind them, filling the courtyard with an eerie scarlet glow. Their colorless faces looked menacing, even from here. Then, one of the men smiled, and they all smiled eerily. Vacant eyes and fake smiles.

I recoiled back into the room in horror. Somewhere nearby, the baby began crying.

"We're leaving. Now." Tracy said, and she began throwing our belongings into our luggage. "Kids, get your shoes on. We're walking out the door in one minute. I don't care if we're in quarantine, they can arrest us or make us quarantine in a different hotel, it doesn't matter. We're getting out of here."

We opened our door and stepped into the hall. The hall was dark. Only one distant light at the far end of the hall was on.

The door to the room across from ours was cracked open. A soft red light glowed around the frame. Inside, we could hear shuffling noises of something approaching the door, moving slowly. Charlotte started backing into our room, shaking her head in fear. I took her hand and we started running down the hall toward the lobby.

As we passed the room next to ours, the door was suddenly struck loudly from the inside. "I have to *get OUT*, I can't *STAY here*," a man's voice roared from the other side. We ran on.

We reached the end of the hall. To our left, the hallway to the main lobby. To the right, another hallway stretched into another wing of the hotel. As we began to head to the lobby, the single light illuminating the hall went out.

Tracy gasped and Will and Charlotte cried out. We pulled each other close in the dark. "We can still make it," I said, trying to keep my voice from shaking. "I can still see the door to the lobby ahead..."

I jumped as a flashlight clicked on, shining in my face.

"Why are you out of your rooms? You must go back, now! Hurry!" It was the front desk clerk. For the first time, he seemed agitated and tense.

I pushed my way past him and we ran to the lobby. The doors to the rooms on both sides of us slowly opened as we passed, pouring red light into the hall. Voices from the rooms called to us, asking and pleading with us to stay. We burst into the lobby, running beneath the chandelier as we made for the exit.

The front door of the hotel had changed. Where it had been an unremarkable, but at least clean and functioning, glass door, it was now stained grey with dust. A rusted metal chain with a padlock was threaded through the handles of both doors. It looked as though it had not been used for many months. I pulled desperately at the handles, but the doors were shut fast. I turned to look back into the lobby.

The clerk was standing by the front desk. "You should return to your room. Guests are not permitted out of their rooms!" His voice increasing in pitch to near hysteria.

I picked up a chair and hurled it into the entrance, shattering the glass. We climbed through carefully and fled down the street.

When the taxi dropped us off at my mom's house on the outskirts of Chicago a couple hours later, she greeted us happily at the door. "I know it's late, but it's just so wonderful to have you all here with me! Let me get a look at you!" She said cheerily.

We were still shaken, and she waited until the kids had settled in bed to ask what had happened. I told her the story of the last two days, and her flushed cheeks went white.

"What's wrong, mom?" I asked.

"That hotel, Whitehall Palace, was shut down almost a year ago. Some 50 or 60 people died there early during the pandemic. Bad sanitation, the HVAC system, I don't know what it was, but the health authorities shut the place down."

"What are you saying?" I looked at her with dawning dread.

"I'm saying that place has been closed and condemned for 12 months. I'm saying, it seems like you were quarantining with ghosts!"

60   SCREAMCATCHER

4

"We make up horrors to help us cope
with the real ones."
-Stephen King

THE DEEP, DARK WOODS

Can you *please* turn off the sound on that thing? This is one of our favorites."

My dad's eyes watched me from the rearview mirror. I rolled my eyes and sighed as theatrically as I could and turned off the volume on my handheld. Dad winked, and he, my mom, and my sister started belting out another Hamilton song. "Sing with us, Dan!" my mom called out. I slouched deeper into the backseat and focused on my game.

"Ugh," I groaned loudly. "You are all so annoying!"

"You used to love musicals, Dan! When did that change?" My mom asked.

Honestly, I didn't know. These days I felt like I was too cool for everyone except my friends. My mom and dad annoyed me, my sister literally drove me crazy. I knew it wasn't fair. I loved my family, especially my parents. They had always been there for me, and if I was honest, so had my sister. But, I guess this was part of becoming a teenager.

We were going camping in the deep woods in northern

Maine and had been driving for a few hours. Our trunk was packed to the ceiling with supplies for a full week in the woods: coolers of eggs and meat and bags of snacks and bread and veggies, jugs of water, piles of wood, and all the camping gear.

I had wanted to stay back with friends, but my dad convinced me to join, saying it would be an adventure and a good story for my friends. Now that we were on the road, and the family was belting out Hamilton, I felt I'd made a huge mistake.

Walls of green blurred by the window. We were heading to Misty Woods, a remote state park that, last week, my dad had enthusiastically described as the "absolute middle of nowhere." He had a habit of getting really excited about stuff that ordinary people would not. It seemed like he had been right, I thought. It had been ages since we had seen another car.

We soon left the main road, pulling on to a dirt lane, and soon after that we turned on to an even smaller, overgrown road with long grass taller than the wheels of our SUV. The trees loomed close on either side, knotted together in thick clumps. A low mist hovered around the base of the trees and settled on the long grass, giving the forest an otherworldly look. True to the name, I thought.

"We're here!" My dad clapped his hands as he parked the car in a small clearing. Only a couple faded trailhead marker signs gave any hint that anyone had ever camped here before. My mom looked around the clearing, a look of rising skepticism plain in her face. My dad, though, could not be discouraged. "Let's get to it folks! We've got a heck of a week ahead, but we've got a lot to do before dark."

"These woods are freaking me out!" My sister said, looking at the trees.

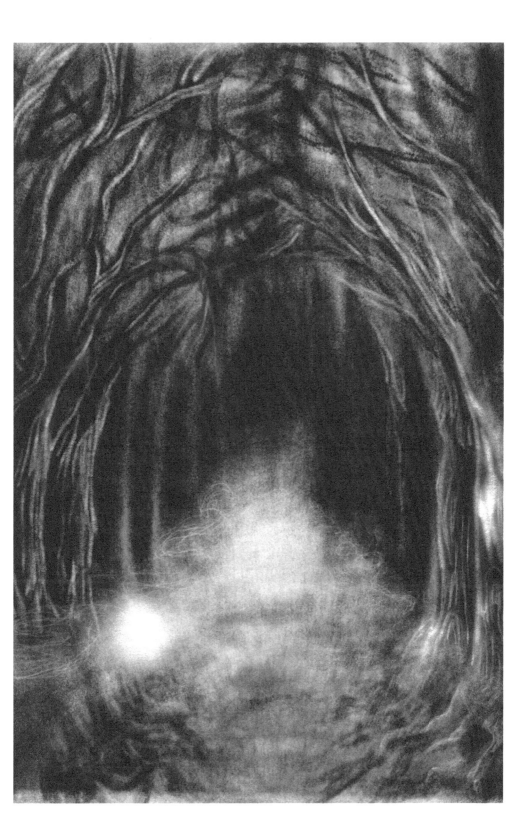

"Don't worry about it," my dad assured us. "Those signs over there mark the path to the campsite. It's supposed to be just a short walk."

As we marched with our gear to the campsite, the mist flowing around our feet, I had to agree with my sister. Though I would never tell her that. Despite it not even being dinner time yet, we had to use our flashlights to illuminate the darkened woods. Huge, gnarled trees pressed tightly together, their roots entangled and spilling on to the narrow path. It was my first time in such a thick forest, long vine-like branches entwined overhead so that it seemed we were walking through a dark tunnel. The cool damp air made the skin on my arms tingle and the hair on the back of my neck stand up.

The walk to the site felt endless. I felt my unease growing with every step. When we arrived at the campsite, I was surprised that I could just make out the outline of our car behind us. Thankfully the site had a firepit and even an ancient picnic table, further proof that we were not the first to wander into this forest. My mom dropped her bags on the table. "I have to say, I think you undersold the spooky mist when you pitched this trip, Walter. Off the grid is one thing, but really?"

My dad, who had seemed a bit subdued during the walk from the car, clapped his hands to reenergize himself. "This is some kind of place, right? I don't know what I was expecting, but it wasn't this! This is going to be a memorable trip, that's for sure." My mom gave him a look, and then started to make the fire. My dad and I set up the tent, while Amara wandered the perimeter, collecting twigs for kindling.

My dad talked to himself as we worked, and I listened to the woods. It was so quiet. Where were the birds? Where was the soft *snap* of deer or other animals moving through the forest? And why did I feel so much like I was *being watched?* I couldn't see anything, couldn't hear anything aside from my dad murmuring and the crackle of my mom's fire, but I felt sure that something was watching us from the woods. From the darkness beyond the trees. Something that had been waiting a long time for new campers to come to this site...

You're freaking yourself out, I told myself. I put the thought from my mind and focused on finishing the tent. I had always been the brave one. Ready for action and adventure, which was part of the reason I agreed to come on this trip. But, this place, there was something strange about these woods.

Later that night, after dinner, our family was feeling more at ease. My dad was telling a scary story around the fire, while we roasted s'mores. It was a tradition for our campouts, and one of my favorites. I loved scary stories, and I *loved* scaring my sister!

"And as it came closer, its red, red eyes opened. Its mouth opened, wider and wider. Its huge hands, matted with mud and fur, reached closer and closer. And then, it let out a... mighty... *ROOOOAR!*" Amara, who had been shrinking further and further into her mom's jacket, eyes as big as golf balls, shrieked. Grabbing her flashlight, she bolted down the trail to the car. I grinned at my dad, who stood up with a look of amusement and concern on his face. Mom shook her head at us in annoyance and turned to jog down the trail to the car where Amara had bolted.

A few moments later: "Walter, come here." My mom was a short way down the trail, her voice a command.

"What is it?" He walked to her, as I stared into the campfire. The fire was large, crackling from the pinecones Amara had thrown in. In the light of the fire, the woods looked like any other campsite. I found myself wondering how the campsite would look later that night, when the fire had died, when we were all asleep. When the creatures of the woods might come wandering in from the dark, wanting a closer look at these new, warm visitors sleeping soundly in their tents...

My parents were whispering furiously to each other. What where they doing? I stood and walked to them.

My dad watched me from the corner of his eyes as I approached, and their voices trailed off. He had a look that I had not seen in his face before. My mom turned and walked quickly to the car to see Cora.

"What's going on..." My voice, too, trailed off, as I saw the shape in the earth near my father's feet, illuminated by my flashlight. A deep impression in the moist ground. A *large* impression, several inches deep at least, deep enough that the mist swirled in it reflected by my flashlight. It was in the shape of a footprint. *Was* it a footprint? It was enormous...

"What is that, Dad?"

He looked at me, the firelight shining off his face. "Let's go check on your sister."

At the car, Mom and Amara were sitting in the backseat, playing Uno by flashlight. Amara seemed to have completely forgotten the story that had scared her at the campfire, as she laughed and made Mom draw more cards. Mom made a big deal of pretending to be angry, drawing each card with as much fake annoyance as she could. The mood in the car felt so normal, so at odds with my rising panic about what we had seen, that I didn't know what to say.

"Let's go make some s'mores!" My dad announced.

"*What?*" I almost shouted. I had had a bad feeling since we had entered these woods, and I was convinced that the

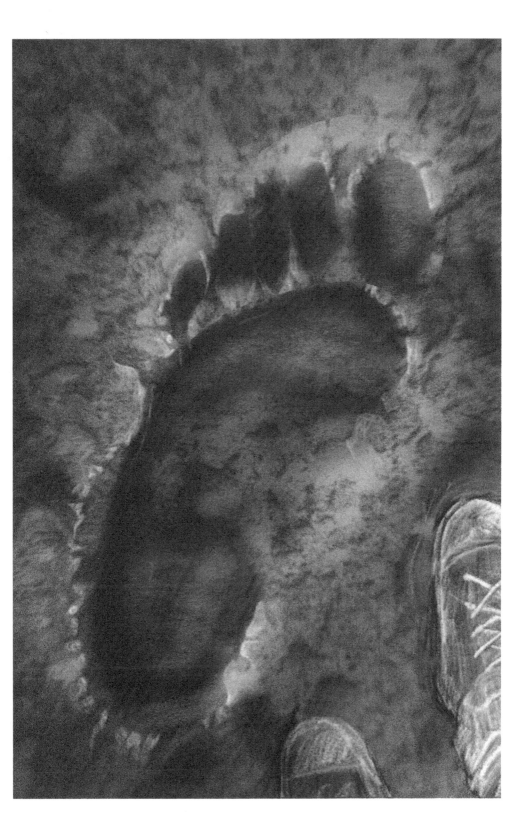

footprint meant it was time to leave. How could my dad want to make s'mores? "Are you kidding?"

"Dan, that mark in the ground could have been anything. It could have been made by some falling branches. The ground is really wet, I don't know, maybe the earth there is sinking a bit and made a funny shape. It's not anything to be worried about. It's certainly not a reason for us to drive all the way home." My mom watched my dad carefully as he talked. I couldn't tell if she agreed or not.

We walked back to the campsite without talking, the flashlights guiding the way. My mom came over to me. "Dan, we can't let fear get the better of us, right? Your dad is probably right that that mark on the ground is nothing. It would be crazy to go home after that long drive! Can you imagine telling your friends that we ran home because we were spooked by a funny looking shape on the ground?" I laughed a little at that. "When we get up in the morning we'll go explore. This place won't be scary at all once we've all slept and the sun is up." My mom was always able to cheer me up. Maybe they were right, I thought.

I woke in the middle of the night. Unsure why I had awoken, I stared up through the tent's mesh roof into the dark branches of the forest above us, listening carefully to the night sounds. Finally, grabbing my flashlight, I stood up and moved as quietly as I could to the tent door.

"What are you doing, Dan?"

My dad was watching me, his head still on his pillow but his eyes wide open. Had he also been listening.

"I want to see what's out there!" I whispered.

"What? It's the middle of the night. Go back to bed."

My dad stared at me for a few moments, when it was clear that I was leaving the tent.

"Fine. You and I can go look around for a few moments. If Bigfoot isn't standing right outside, then we're going back to bed. You need to sleep." He was clearly annoyed to have to get out of his cozy sleeping bag.

I felt a jolt of fear. Even though I had been just about to go out into the night, doing it made my fear much more real. I slowly opened the tent flap, and we stepped outside.

The mist flowed around our feet. Even though it was a full moon tonight, only the slightest light from the moon filtered its way through the tangle of branches above. The clearing was *dark*. Not nighttime dark, but the dark of a cold basement, of a deep cave. I could only just make out the outline of the trees that surrounded us.

I turned on my flashlight and walked back toward the footprint we had seen earlier. I found it quickly and shone the light around, not sure what I was looking for. Something on a nearby tree caught my eye. I walked closer, my feet squelching in the wet earth. Something was on the side of the tree... claw marks? No, it was something carved. Writing.

IT COMES AT NIGHT

I stood, frozen, for what felt like hours, my flashlight pointed at the message on the tree. The night suddenly felt colder. The dark felt like it was pressing against my skin. What comes?

"Maggie, Amara, wake up. We need to leave. Right now." I heard my dad behind us, speaking urgently through the tent flap.

I finally turned, and from this distance my flashlight illuminated the whole campsite. It looked like a hurricane had come through the site. Our cooler had been overturned, its contents emptied and strewn across the clearing. Our bags of snacks and granola bars and other things had been torn open, the food partially devoured. And everywhere, huge footprints were sunk into the earth. A maze of massive footprints, made by something huge that had ransacked our camp.

My mom and sister were groggily emerging from the tent while my dad shone his flashlight into the trees around us, sweeping the beam back and forth. The close trees made it hard to see into the forest. Shadows thrown by our flashlights created huge dark shapes that loomed over the clearing.

A large branch snapped in the woods. All four of us spun toward the noise. The flashlights showed nothing but a wall of trees. Another branch snapped, closer. My dad and I moved our flashlights back and forth, searching for the origin of the sound. My mom and Amara stood holding each other, eyes wide.

"Go to the car. Go to the car!" My dad said, and we all ran through the tunnel of trees. What had been a short walk yesterday felt endless. Branches and twigs snapped nearby as something moved through the forest toward us but always out of sight. Underneath the sound I thought I could hear something deeper, a low guttural grunting of some huge beast...

We reached the car and, as my dad fought with his keys, I turned back. Framed by the tunnel of trees and branches that led back to our campsite, I saw a tall human like shape. Two reddish embers glowed where its eyes were. No animal I had ever seen had such eyes. My flashlight fell from my hand.

The shape lumbered toward us. In the faint moonlight I could barely make out its body, but its arms seemed longer than a human's, its body and legs seemed thick and heavy.

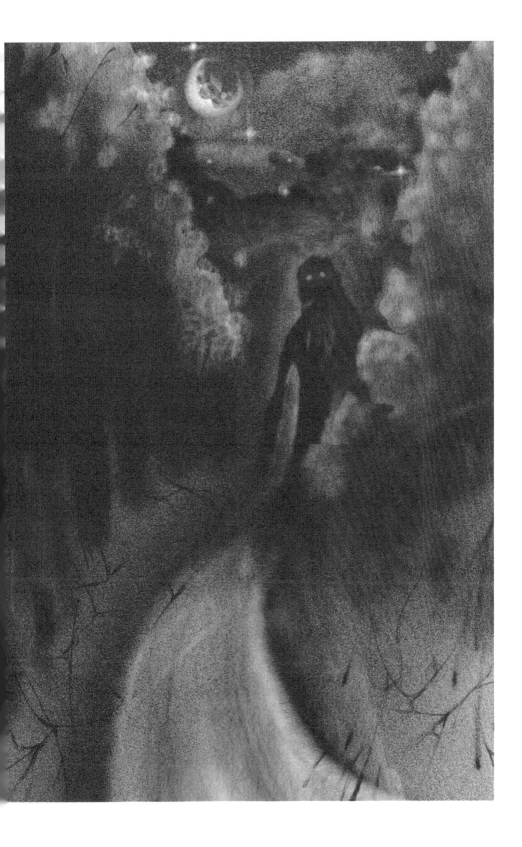

I watched the two red embers come closer and closer, and I imagined what the huge hungry mouth below those eyes would look like. It grunted as it took another step with its huge monstrous feet.

My mom pulled me into the car behind me and slammed the door shut. My dad put the car into reverse, and we pulled onto the path that led out of the forest. My heart was still thundering in my chest as I felt a wave of relief sweep over me. Thoughts raced through my head. I was grateful to be with my family! We were going home. I couldn't wait to get back to school and tell my friends what had happened. They would never believe me.

I looked back through the rear window. For just a moment, I thought I could see the towering shape of the creature standing in the park road behind us, its burning eyes watching our truck speed away.

5

"I was never one who believed in monsters.
Until I was proven, by humans, that they exist."
-C.R. Bittar

MOTHER?

We barely made it to the gate on time. Mom had left her carryon bag at Starbucks, and so we had had to frantically run through the airport like we were in some kind of movie. Typical of my mom. She was always forgetting things these days. With dad gone, no one reminded her. Not that I was any better. In fact, I was pretty sure that I was just like her. In my own world, my dad used to say. Until that drunk driver had killed him last year.

We were the last to board. The flight attendant made a point of letting my mom know that she had almost missed the plane. My sister of course had all of our documents neatly organized and ready for boarding. She was two years younger than me, but already more organized than both my mom and I, and more observant. Nothing could get past Samia. I couldn't stand that. It drove me crazy, actually. My mom always told us that Samia was our scientist and I was the movie star with the over active imagination.

Mom had been nervous about this trip. It was the first trip

since dad died, and it was a big one: we were going across the world, from Tokyo to NYC. We were traveling to stay with our grandparents, who we hadn't seen since the funeral.

We got to our seats and settled in. Mom took the aisle, and Samia the window. I liked being closer to mom, so I didn't care that I had the middle seat. She made me feel safe. Samia was already on her Switch, and I poked the screen in front of me, wondering how I would possibly get through the endless flight ahead. Mom had her earbuds in, probably listening to a podcast. Something about healing after grief, or finding purpose after tragedy, or something like that. She listened to a lot of them these days. I think it was helping, but I wasn't sure. She still cried all the time.

Two hours passed. The featureless ocean below made it look like we were barely moving. My screen said we still had twelve hours to go. Mom said we could watch a movie after we ate but then we all needed to try to sleep. The meal service was fine. Not great, but fine, and I started watching some superhero movie. My sister fell asleep quickly, and pretty soon mom was asleep too, snoring softly. It seemed like most people on the plane had the same idea, and soon the cabin was dark and quiet.

I really had to pee, but I didn't want to wake mom up. I looked longingly at the bathrooms. Standing by the bathroom I noticed a woman. Was she looking at me? It was hard to tell, her face hard to make out in the dark cabin. She reminded me of my mom, with the same reddish hair and same height. She even seemed to be dressed like my mom. I felt increasingly uneasy as she stood there for a few moments. I didn't know why, but I was sure she was looking at me. Then the woman turned and went into the toilet.

Mom seemed completely passed out, her head hanging forward. I nudged my sister to try to wake her up and tell her what I'd seen.

"What?" she said groggily, super annoyed that I'd woken her up. I told her quickly what I saw, and she rolled her eyes and turned away, trying to go back to sleep. I waited for the bathroom door to open again. But when the woman emerged, she looked nothing like my mom. She walked past my aisle without noticing me, and I saw that she had blonde hair and was pretty tall. Was I just really tired? I turned to watch the woman take her seat a few rows behind.

I leaned against mom, feeling instantly better from her warmth. I watched my movie and gradually fell into a fitful sleep. I had strange, unsettling dreams, searching for something but never finding it. What had I lost?

I woke up with a gasp. The flight attendant was asking me something. The feeling of having lost something was still in my gut. It was light outside. How long did I sleep?

The flight attendant, looking tired and annoyed, again asked if I wanted a sandwich. I got a chicken sandwich and noticed then that Mom wasn't in her seat. I asked Samia, who was again crouched over her Switch, where she'd gone.

"Where do you think?" She said with her usual snark.

I waited for my mom. The bathroom door opened and Mom walked over, giving me a big, wide smile as she approached. Her teeth gleamed under the lights of the cabin. I rubbed the sleep from my eyes as she sat in her seat.

"How did you sleep, my little gumdrop?" Mom asked, her eyes crinkling with her smile. The feeling in my stomach from my dream still hadn't gone away, and I thought for a moment that maybe I still was dreaming. Something felt... different.

"I feel so rested!" Mom enthused, stretching her arms wide and putting one arm around my shoulder to give me a hug. She was still looking at me with her toothy grin, and I gave her a small smile back. Her hand on my arm felt cold and smooth. For some reason I thought of sharks. I looked at Samia, who was absorbed in her game.

"Mom, where are your glasses?" She had been wearing them earlier. She always wore her glasses on long flights, so she didn't have to change her contacts.

"I just put in my contacts. We'll be landing soon!" Her smile faded and she turned her face away, taking her arm back. She began drumming her fingers on her knees. Her nails were red. When did she paint her nails? Had they been like that last night? I couldn't remember.

The pilot announced we were beginning our descent into New York. Samia finally looked up and pressed her face against the window. I wanted to get her attention, but I didn't know what to say. Even though Mom was looking away, I could feel her focus on me. Her presence, which I usually found so comforting, felt suffocating. Something was wrong.

She began gathering her things from under the seat in front of her. She glanced at me, and I saw that her normally green eyes seemed darker, bluer than I remembered. Our eyes met and she gave me a strange smile, drawing back her upper lip so I could again see her shining teeth. Had they gotten longer, pointier?

"My eyes are feeling pretty dry after that long flight, my pet," she said in a sweet voice. She sounded like my mom. She *was* my mom, but... she had never called me "pet" before. I felt a slowly rising panic.

"...Mom? Did you change clothes?" Samia had turned

away from the window and I could see immediately that she, too, sensed something was wrong. I saw what she was talking about: the cherry red sweater she had been wearing earlier now seemed darker, a bloody red shade that matched her fingernails.

Mom leaned forward, her face inches from my own. "Buckle up, my pets. The last thing we want is for someone to get *hurt* after this long, long journey." She clicked my seat buckle, humming to herself. I looked at Samia and could see my panic reflected in her eyes!

I shut my eyes and gripped the arms of my seat as the plane landed. This must be a dream, I thought, though I knew that it was very real.

We started deboarding the plane. Mom kept humming tunelessly, putting a strong, cold hand on each of our shoulders as she guided us down the aisle to depart the plane. My fear began to boil over. This was not my mother. This was some other mother, some copy of my mother. If we left, what would happen to us? *Where was Mom?* I tried to stall and slow our exit from the plane, but the other mother's iron grip pushed me forward.

We walked down the ramp and into the terminal. I looked up at the other mother, who gazed down at me with glee in her eyes. "I cannot *wait* to get you two home," she murmured, a smile revealing a mouth of teeth that had grown small and very, very sharp.

I stumbled in horror, gripping Samia's hand. As I took another step forward, trying to get out of the other mother's tight grasp, I looked out the window back to the now empty plane we had just left. In one window, I saw our Mom, her face pressed to the glass, soundlessly crying out to us.

6

"A flower blooming in the desert,
proves to the world, that adversity,
no matter how great, can be overcome."
-Matshona Dhliwayo

THE ABANDONED TENT

hreds of the tattered tent billowed in the desert wind. A smoldering, blackened firepit was nearby, ashes scattered around the campsite. Through the flaps of the tent I could see dirty blankets, stained with reddish-brown spots and covered with sand. The site seemed like it had been abandoned for weeks, but a thin curl of smoke rose from the firepit.

"Well, that's the weirdest thing I've seen on this drive," my mom said through gritted teeth, gripping the handlebar on the roof of our SUV as the car rattled and bounced and slid its way across the desert. "Should we stop for directions?"

"*Al-Sahliyya*... do not go too far, *ya binti*. The deep desert is home to no one. Only *Al-Sahliyya*." The warning of the Bedouin in the village echoed in my ears. I had been standing by the car, bored while my dad let air out of our tires, when the Bedouin had approached me. His pale eyes peered out at me, his skin hardened brown by the desert, wrapped in a keffiyeh. "*Al-Sahliyya*... do not go too far," he had said. I had immediately gotten back in the car. Now, we had been driving three hours into the desert and hadn't seen a soul for almost the entire time.

"Who knows," my dad said, his voice wobbling from the vibrations of our car. "There's Bedouin out here herding camels somewhere. They probably stop here for rest sometimes. Anyway, we're practically to our site." He rapped the GPS with his knuckle.

Sure enough, minutes later he pulled our SUV into a

narrow wadi, with tall rock walls on both sides that provided relief from the sun. We were in Wadi Rum in Jordan, beginning a three-day campout. My brother, our dog Luna, and I agreed, it was going to be epic. We were prepared for anything: we had traction pads to get unstuck from the sand, a satellite phone, a telescope, flares, a huge first aid kit, and fully stocked coolers. I had loved every minute of the drive, even despite the Bedouin's warning. Wadi Rum's dunes, red sand, and rocky plateaus made me feel like I was living a movie.

The site was perfect, but I did not like that I could still see, on a distant hillside, the abandoned tent. I did not like that at all. Then...

"Something's moving at the camp," I said.

"Yeah. Sure," my brother said, rolling his eyes. "I'm sure they're setting up for a big party."

Was I wrong? I was sure I had seen something, for a brief moment. Large. Moving behind the tent on the hillside. I watched for a minute longer, but saw nothing.

We set up our tents and the fire, Luna running around joyfully, smelling old campers and goat hair and camel bones. The site had obviously been used before, with a few old plastic bottles and tin foil caught in the desert scrub. Trained after years of Scouts, my brother and I swept the site to clean up trash while my parents unpacked.

I walked out toward the entrance of the wadi, picking up garbage while Luna followed close on my heels. Looking out into the desert, the red sand hills in front of me were framed by vertical cliffs of rock that looked almost like it was melting under Jordan's hot sun. It was otherworldly. The only sound I could hear was the wind. I closed my eyes for a moment to breathe in the calmness of the desert, but when I reopened them I again saw the tent, far off. Even from here I see it tilting to the side in the strong gusts. I squinted, trying to see if the black shape was there. I thought maybe it was, inside the tent, looking back toward me. I shivered, despite the heat.

That evening was hot dogs, s'mores, and ghost stories around the fire. My brother, I had to admit, was an epic teller of ghost stories, and though I would never tell him I was looking forward to his tale. When he started launching into a story of a haunted tent, however, I asked him to stop.

"Seriously, Jenna. Get a grip! Let's get out the telescope, we can take a look at your spooky scary tent and then maybe find some planets."

We walked to the entrance of the wadi. It was a moonless night—my parents had planned it that way—and the dome of stars above us was unbelievable. The campfire behind us seemed like a miniscule island of light in an ocean of darkness. I started to set up the telescope.

"Whoa! Do you see that?" Ameer asked. I looked up, hoping I hadn't missed a shooting star. His finger pointed instead outward, away from our wadi, back the way we had come. I looked, and I saw it. There was a fire at the abandoned campsite.

"See? I told you there was someone there," I said angrily to my brother.

My dad took the telescope and aimed it at the site. "Yep, there's a fire going. Some of those camel herders, I'm sure. I don't really see them around right now, though."

"Ok, enough spying, let's see if we can find Mars." My mom grabbed the telescope from his hands.

I stayed with the telescope after my family grew bored and returned to the campfire. I had wanted to wait so that I could avoid my brother's derision. I turned the telescope to the distant campsite. I found the fire. Now a metal rod had been extended over the fire, and meat of some sort was impaled on that rod. I gently moved the telescope, searching for the tent. There it was: the torn and thin canvas flapping like a filthy flag, as creepy as ever.

Something moved inside the tent, a dark shape, emerging from the other side and leaving the view of the telescope. I scrambled to move the telescope back to the fire, over-adjusting and losing focus, and a minute went by as I worked to align the lens. The fire came back into focus. A large figure shrouded in a brown cloak was facing the fire, its back to the telescope. Its shoulders were incredibly wide, the hood enormous.

A hand reached out to turn the spit over the fire. Even in the flickering firelight, I could see the greenish tint of its hand, encrusted with scabs or scales. Thick, sharp claws extended from each finger.

That night, I slept fitfully. I kept dreaming of monsters, and in the hours before dawn, I woke with a start.

Apart from the wind, I had heard nothing all night. But now, a soft steady sound, the sound of something being dragged through the sand, came to my ears. I lay with my eyes wide, staring at my black tent wall in front of me. Was the sound from nearby? The desert's emptiness carried sound a long way, and I couldn't even tell what direction it was coming from. I held my flashlight in my shaking hands, carefully avoiding turning it on.

Eventually the sound passed, and I lay awake for the rest of the night.

In the morning, Luna was gone. We called out to him, rattling his food bowl. At the entrance to the wadi, my brother cried out to us and we ran over. There was blood in the sand, red against red. The droplets were in a long, twisting trail through the sand, made by something that had wended its way through the desert scrub. The trail wound its way into the distance. Looking further out, I saw the ruined campsite on its distant hill.

My parents' faces went white when they saw the blood. "A... maybe, a fox? A large fox?" My dad murmured to himself.

"Get the keys. We need to follow the trail." My mom said, looking hard at my dad.

"Yes, let's go now. Get in the car."

We drove into the desert, my dad driving slowly alongside the winding path made through the sand. Small patches of blood dotted the sand. We didn't talk. We all knew what each other was thinking, but no one wanted to be the first to say it. With no surprise, I saw that the blood trail had led us to the base of the abandoned tent's hill.

We climbed to the summit together, unsure what we would find. I saw that my dad had taken out his hunting knife. We walked cautiously up to the abandoned tent. The firepit nearby still smoldered, the metal spit in the sand to the side, and no sign of the meat from the night before. Up close, I could see that the tent was spattered with reddish-brown drops. My dad pushed the shredded tent flap to the side with the tip of his knife, and I heard his sharp intake of breath.

A huge serpentine creature was curled on the floor of the tent. Its skin was mottled many shades of sickly green. Its body was long and thick, tapering to a heavy, triangular head like that of a crocodile. Its eyes were shut, and its breath blew small puffs of sand in the tent. I noticed with revulsion

that one of its short, muscular arms was openly bleeding from what appeared like bite marks. The blood was trickling down on to the sand, which was covered in bones and bits of cloth.

Pinned to the sand under the creature's claws was Luna, his eyes open and petrified. He looked to us and whimpered.

I was frozen. My dad reached forward with a trembling hand. Luna licked it, squirming under the weight of the creature's claws. I could see the whites of his eyes. My dad, using the flat of his blade, gently lifted one of the creature's talons, allowing Luna to bolt from the tent, covered in sand and dirt. The creature stirred but continued to sleep.

We raced down the hill, taking huge giant strides down the loose sand. Luna piled into the car next to us, still trembling from his ordeal.

Later that day, we drove into the village. We had decided we had had enough of the desert. As we waited to refill the tires, the Bedouin I had seen the previous day came up to my window. His pale eyes looked into mine and we held each other's gaze. He knew. His face split into a huge grin, though his eyes did not smile. "You are lucky, *binti*. Few have walked away from *Al-Sahliyya*. Very few."

7

"Fear is the path to the Dark Side.
Fear leads to anger, anger leads to hate,
hate leads to suffering."
-Yoda

THE INTRUDER

Saturday morning light streamed through my window. I groaned and rolled toward the wall. No fun Saturday night lay ahead. "Ugh... I hate babysitting," I mumbled into my pillow. My mom had basically begged me to babysit my sister, Jamie, and her friend, Rosa, for the evening so she and Rosa's mom could go to dinner and a movie. Rosa's dad wasn't in the picture anymore, at least that's how my mom put it. No Rosa's dad, no fun for Kelley, I thought.

We lived in an apartment complex down the street from my dad's office. He owned the business and worked late a lot. My mom, on the other hand, was super social and took all of five minutes to make friends with the entire apartment complex. Usually, I liked that about my mom, but lately it had been annoying. I turned 12 a month ago, so mom's friend network had become my network of employers, as my mom had decided I needed summer work experience as a babysitter for half the building.

The money was nice, yeah, and raiding the neighbors'

refrigerators and freezers for sweets was kind of great, but I wasn't sure if I even liked babysitting. The kids didn't bother me but it was kind of creepy staying in the apartments alone after the kids went to bed, waiting for the parents to come back. Or more often, call to say they would be late. Most evenings, I didn't even walk back to my apartment until midnight. Even though it was my apartment building, it felt like a different place at night. The halls felt longer. Distant noises echoing through the halls. I definitely didn't like that part.

I rolled out of bed and wandered to the bathroom. After getting dressed, I ate and sat on the couch next to Jamie. Her eyes were wide and glassy, drinking in the Saturday morning cartoons. She was three years younger than me and she had learned early that Saturday morning was the only time in the week my parents let us watch screens as much as we wanted. I don't think I had ever gotten up before her on a Saturday.

Sitting next to her, I opened my book and began my morning ritual of reading. I loved to read, and even better my mom loved to see me read, so I could often delay morning chores by hours.

After a while, my mom and dad emerged from their bedroom. "Can you make me breakfast?" Jamie asked, her eyes riveted to the screen. My mom rolled her eyes and went to the kitchen.

After Jamie had eaten, the list of chores was unveiled. My reading had not bought me much time today. "Please be done by 1, we need to go to the mall so I can buy a shirt for tonight," Mom said.

I hated the mall. The lights made me tired and had a sterile smell like a hospital. "Hard pass," I replied, picking up my book.

"You need to come with me, Kelley, because I want you to start thinking about school clothes. School will be here before you know it!" she said cheerily.

"Thank God," my dad quipped, "You both need to get back to school!" I stuck my tongue out at him.

"Oh, David, it's been nice having them home. You agree, even if you won't say it." My mom smiled at my dad. He poked out his tongue back at me.

I didn't even want to think about school. While I liked being with friends, and the classes were fine, middle school was hard. I was growing up in all sorts of weird ways, and I felt lately that my body was betraying me. The body I knew as a kid, well, it had definitely been changing, and I wasn't sure I was ready to be the "young lady" that my mom had begun referring to me as over the past month. "Fine. But I'm getting another hoodie." I said, staring hard at mom to make sure she knew I was serious.

After cleaning and shopping, Saturday slipped away. We walked into the house at five, and mom told Jamie and I to get ready to head to Rosa's. My dad was gone, probably at work already, and wouldn't be home for a long time.

"Why can't Rosa come here?" I asked, annoyed. "Mix things up?"

"Kelley, babysitting in this apartment complex is a gift. You are getting great experience, and you can walk to your job! That never happens. Plus, you're getting paid. This is your first job. You go to your job. The job doesn't come to you."

I groaned and went to grab another book and my journal. I hated it when my mom is right. Best not to give her the satisfaction of hearing it.

My mom made a quick dinner of cheese quesadillas, baby carrots and milk. By six, the three of us were on the way to Rosa's.

"Can we watch a scary movie?" Jamie asked, looking up at me.

"I doubt it," I said.

"Kelley, when you talk to kids," mom began, in her best preachy voice, "you need to say yes or no and why. Not "I doubt it." If you do that, you are asking for bargaining, and from experience, that's not a fun place to be as a caregiver."

"Okay, then, no, Jamie, you can't watch a scary movie at Rosa's. You hate them. You say that like them, and then you freak out before the movie even starts. And, you and Rosa won't be able to sleep." I rolled my eyes.

"I saw that," mom said.

"What time will you guys get back tonight?" Jamie was a master at suddenly changing the subject.

"Too late for you, honey, and you are spending the night, remember? The movie ends at 10:30, so it won't be any earlier than 11."

"I'm definitely not staying the night." I said flatly.

"That's fine, I'll come by when we're back, and we can walk home together." I tried to mask my relief as mom walked up to knock on Rosa's door.

Rosa's mom ran down the list of babysitter to-dos, which if I'm being honest, isn't much.

...Put the dishes in the dishwasher, don't let her have sweets, she can have popcorn during the movie, careful to not burn it, it burns fast, make sure she washes up before bed, she

has to brush her teeth too, watch that she brushes behind their teeth, she always forgets that, make sure she is in bed by 9, you can read a story if you want, there's some food in the fridge if you're hungry....

I smiled internally, thinking that at least I'd have a lot of time for reading and journaling.

After mom and her friend left, I gave Rosa her dinner. Jamie was searching for cartoons on the TV. Soon they wandered off to Rosa's room to play, and I cleaned up the kitchen. "Kids, go get your PJs on!. Then let's watch that movie," I yelled upstairs to Rosa and Jamie. I got the popcorn started as I waited for them to come back down.

Our apartments, and all the apartments in this complex, shared the same layout, though the side of the building opposite from our apartment had apartments with a mirrored design. I always felt uneasy and a little off on this side of the building. The living room was to the left rather than the right, even though it looked identical. The stairs were in the same place, leading upstairs to two bedrooms with onsuite bathrooms, though they were on the wrong side of the hallway like I was in some bizarro dimension. As I yelled again upstairs for the kids to get ready, I felt like even the sound of my voice seemed wrong, bouncing off the walls in strange ways.

I yelled again up the stairs, and finally Rosa and Jamie emerged in their PJs. "You ready?" I asked.

"Yes!" They came running down, jumping down the last couple steps and plopping onto the sofa. "Thanks for the popcorn, Kelley!" Rosa said, flipping on the movie.

When the movie ended, I sent the kids back upstairs to brush and wash, overriding their protests. If there was one thing I was firm on with babysitting, it was bedtimes. I could see my future, only minutes away, with the refrigerator and freezer at my fingertips.

I was reading their second nighttime story, the girls pressed against me on both sides, when Rosa looked up, her eyes wide. "Do you hear that?"

I stopped the story to ask her what she means, but then I heard it too. The door was rattling downstairs.

"You mom must be home early!" I said, as I got up and walked to the stairs.

The door rattled again as I stood at the top of the stairs. From the upstairs landing I could just see the doorknob, which was being turned back and forth. I could see the light of the downstairs living room reflecting off the knob. It didn't sound like Rosa's mom trying to fit a key in the lock, I thought. Why would they be home so early? They should be in the middle of their movie...

Suddenly, the door shook as whoever was on the other side threw themselves against it. A heavy thud reverberated through the apartment. Rosa and Jamie, who were huddled right behind me, both screamed and ran back into Rosa's room. I could hear them slam the bathroom door. At almost the same time, the front door again creaked on its hinges.

I turned and ran back into Rosa's room. The bathroom door was locked. "Girls!" I whisper-yelled, "Let me in." I could feel my heart pounding in my chest. Heat was rising in my face. I pounded the flat of my hand on the door. *"Open the door!"* I could hear panic creeping into my voice. Another thud came from downstairs, with a sound like splintering wood.

"Kelley, call mom." It sounded like Rosa had her mouth right against the other side of door. "Yes! Call mom! Or dad," Jamie echoed from deeper in the bathroom. My phone! Where did I put my phone? With a sick feeling in my gut I pictured clearly my phone sitting on the kitchen counter, downstairs.

I was frozen. I had never been so scared. I could hear the door downstairs, clearly splintering now, thuds coming more frequently as the intruder seemed to be becoming more excited with each blow. Should I lock myself in the room? No - Rosa's mom had removed the locks, I remembered her talking about it the last time I had babysat. The room had a window and we were on the second floor... but I couldn't leave the girls. I had to call for help.

I remembered seeing an old landline phone in Rosa's mom's room. But I was still paralyzed. I would have to run across the upstairs landing, in full view of the front door, to get to the phone. What if I didn't make it in time? What if the intruder saw me and came upstairs?

The girls' sobbing in the bathroom broke my indecision. "Girls, keep the door locked and stay quiet. I am going to call for help." I ran from the bathroom door across the hallway to Rosa's mom's room. As I did so, a shocking crash came from downstairs, as the front door broke inward. From the corner of my eye I saw the dark shape of the intruder taking a step over the ruins of the door. I grabbed the phone from the bedside table, thankful for its long cord, and I ran into the bathroom, shutting and locking the door behind me.

I could barely breath as I pressed 9-1-1.

"Operator 42957, what is your emergency?" The woman on the phone sounded calm and almost bored.

I whispered, "There's an intruder in the house, I mean, the apartment. Not my apartment, where I'm babysitting.

They've broken the front door, they're in the house. There's two other girls here too, they're locked in a different room. We need help, please, hurry." The words came out in a rush as I crawled into the tub, pulling the shower curtain behind me.

"Slow down, honey!" She no longer sounded bored. "Where are you exactly?"

I could hear glass shattering downstairs. My mind was blank. Where was I? "I don't know. I can't remember!" I was choking back sobs. My mind was an empty void, filled only with flashing panic. "We're in... San Antonio, it's an apartment building, we're on, um, oh my god, I'm sorry, I don't know..."

"It's okay, honey," she said calmly. "You're doing great. We are tracing the call and will know your location in a few minutes. The police are coming, just try to stay calm."

I realized that it has been quiet in the apartment for what seemed like ages. Was it only a few seconds? I strained to listen. I covered the earpiece of the phone for a moment to block out the sound of the policewoman's soothing words.

A faint creaking sound. I knew that sound. My apartment made that sound too - the intruder was coming up the stairs.

"I think he's coming closer," I whispered, clenching the phone.

"Stay put. Make sure the door is locked. Don't make a sound. You will be ok, honey, the police are on their way. Stay with me now," she said, her voice firm.

The footsteps entered the bedroom. They paused, a moment of silence stretching to eternity, and then came closer. I forgot to breathe. My chest felt locked in place. The bathroom doorknob rattled, once, and then again. The policewoman said something but I couldn't understand her words. On the other side of the door the intruder chuckled softly, a sound that sent a shiver down my spine.

"Hon, are you still..." The policewoman began, and then the line went dead. The intruder had pulled the phone line from the wall.

The dead phone in my hand, I curled in the bathtub, listening to the doorknob rattle. I felt like I was in a daze. What would happen when the door opened? There was no doubt the intruder would get in—the bathroom door was much thinner than the front door. My mind generated image after image of the shadow on the other side of the door, all making the same soft chuckle as the door swung open.

Footsteps again. But this time, footsteps away, moving quickly, and heavy creaks as the intruder descended the stairs. The silence was deafening. I could hear my blood pulsing in my ears.

Minutes or maybe years later, I heard shouts of "police!" downstairs. Many footsteps, spreading through the apartment. I felt a heavy rush of gratitude and called out to let them know where I was. I waited in the bathroom until they completed their search of the apartment, and when I finally emerged, Jamie and Rosa came running into my arms, and we all started crying.

Later that evening, with my mom, dad, and Rosa's mom sitting in the living room, we were finally completing our interviews with the police. Jamie and Rosa were asleep, curled up on the couch. It was now well past midnight, and my heartbeat was finally returning to normal.

An officer said, "This seems like a standard burglary. Whoever it was came in, took the TV in the living room and busted up some stuff in the kitchen, and then came looking for Ms. Garcia's valuables. They took what they could and left. Perhaps the intruder heard us coming, otherwise he might have stuck around a bit longer. I don't think there's any reason to think he intended to harm anyone. Though," he said, looking kindly at me, "I know it was a very scary night. You handled yourself very well, miss."

Somehow his words didn't comfort me.

A few days later, we found out the intruder had been Rosa's dad, upset over the divorce and seeking to steal back what he thought was his. I looked at my mom after she told me. "I'm never babysitting again."

She nodded in agreement and reached out to give me a big hug.

8

"The woods are lovely, dark and deep.
But I have promises to keep,
and miles to go before I sleep."
-Robert Frost

THE HIKE

The trail stretched before us, winding its way through trees and brush. Sunlight glinted off of the lake on my left. It was a crisp spring day. My breath misted the air. We were about an hour into the hike, and I was wishing I was anywhere else.

This was Deep Woods Lake State Park. According to my dad it was a brand-new park with brand new trails, which apparently was something to be excited about. He was obsessed with finding new places to hike and explore. He seemed to spend every minute he wasn't at work planning our next hike, or buying camping gear, or strategizing new ways to stuff his pack.

It was Saturday morning. Normal kids slept in on Saturdays, and when they woke up, they could talk to their friends and play video games. Normal kids would watch some TV and laze on the couch and chill out after a long week of school. They did not wake up two hours before sunrise to drive to some random lake in the middle of nowhere. But here I was.

"Anyone need to stop for a drink? Let's stop for a second," my dad said. "Isn't this park just terrific?" He grinned back at us as he rummaged through his pack for water. The trail was about seven miles around the lake, so we had maybe three more hours to go.

"I have to pee," my brother muttered, and he wandered into the brush.

"It really is a beautiful trail," my mom said. "Honestly, I can't say I've ever seen trees like this in Wisconsin. And all the flowers! Just gorgeous."

"Yeah. I've never seen anything like it, honestly. I've never even seen some of these types of flowers before. We'll have to talk to the park rangers when we get back." My dad was a biologist at the University of Madison. He studied mushrooms, which was about the most embarrassing job a parent could have. He loved to tell my friends that he put the "fun" in fungus, which wasn't even the worst of his mushroom jokes. Thank goodness my mom was normal, a high school teacher. She at least probably would not embarrass me if I had her class next year. I was still in middle school in 8th grade, and my brother was a 5th grader.

Mom walked over to dad and put an arm around him. "Maybe someone just planted some unusual flowers here to see if they could grow." She kissed his ear, and he smiled at her.

They both still treated each other like high school sweethearts. Ugh. It was gross.

"Maybe... I'm pretty sure some of these flowers aren't native to the US. At least, I've never seen them before. And look at those trees! You can't tell me that some local decided to plant and raise non-native trees just for fun." Dad was getting animated. "I'm going to talk to Al and Evelyn at the university when we get back. I bet they'll want to come and look at this. Perhaps there's something in the environment here that is shaping the growth around the lake."

"It's not like everything in the world has been discovered already," I said. Thinking about my friends having a relaxed Saturday morning was making me feel argumentative. "I'm sure there's stuff in Wisconsin that hasn't been discovered yet. I mean, it's a new park, right?"

Too late, I realized that my comment only was getting Dad more fired up. I could see him shifting into Dr. Mushroom Professor mode. "That's true, Aren, there remain some flora and fauna around the world that certainly have not been discovered yet. We certainly have not uncovered all of the planet's mysteries. Just think that only a couple decades ago we discovered that the largest lifeform in the world was a fungus living right under our noses in Oregon! Who knows..." he trailed off as he wandered over to inspect some mushrooms at the side of the trail. Three more hours, I thought. Just three.

I took a closer look at the woods around us. Honestly, I hadn't really been paying attention. I had been listening to my headphones for most of the last hour. The woods were different, I thought. The trees and grass were shockingly green, almost emerald, like pictures I'd seen of Ireland. The trees were curved and strange, making me think of Dr. Seuss books. No two were alike, and their bark was a smooth reddish color that I hadn't seen before. They cast a heavy shadow over the path. And the flowers! On both sides of the path, stretching beyond sight into the trees, was a rainbow of small, delicate flowers. I'd seen colorful flowers like that in my neighbor's garden, but out in the middle of the woods?

My dad was filling up a sandwich bag with mushrooms. "Can you believe this! I've never seen this kind of mushroom before in my life. Incredible!"

"What's with all the flowers?" My brother said, yawning, as he emerged from the woods. "Can we eat yet?"

After snacking on power bars and fruit, we continued on the trail. The walk was more interesting now, and it seemed like every minute one of us pointed out a tree or plant or bush that seemed exotic. Even the light seemed different from previous hikes; the sunlight reflecting off the lake into the trees seemed to filter the woods in a hazy green. The air felt thick and smelled of growth and rot. I could see my parents excitedly talking to each other, but I had turned up my music on my headphones.

When dad had been outlining the plan for the hike on the drive up this morning, he mentioned that there was supposed to be a big flat rock at about the halfway point of the hike. We were planning to have lunch there. I thought we should be reaching it pretty soon, though we were moving slower than we usually did on our hikes.

The trail wound lazily through the small hills around the lake. We had to be almost to the rock, I thought. I looked back and saw dad wandering in the bushes along the side of the path, murmuring to himself, while mom was on her knees examining what seemed like a new type of flower. My brother was barely even in sight, he was moving so slowly along the path. I pulled off my headphones.

"Look at the colors!" Mom exclaimed, running her hand over a brightly colored fern. Its leaves were tipped in bright red, and several long yellow and orange tendrils growing from the middle swayed gently in the wind. Her eyes seemed glassy with enthusiasm. "Have you ever seen anything like it? They look like glass..."

I hadn't seen anything like it, but I didn't want to encourage them. I was starving and needed to get to the rock. "Do you mind if I run ahead? I'll stop at that rock and eat and wait for you there. You are SO slow." Neither mom or dad gave any sign they had heard me. Dad was also on his knees, filling another bag with mushrooms.

"Whatever. I will see you at the rock!" I said loudly, and put my headphones back on. I started moving more quickly down the path.

I got to the rock fifteen minutes later. It was huge, sloping down the hillside to the lakefront. The trail led up on to the rock, and I walked down to the edge above the water, looking out over the lake and the wonderland of strange trees and other growth that surrounded it. This was a special place, I thought. I guess this wasn't the worst way to spend a Saturday.

I tore through my lunch, devouring my sandwich, another power bar, and an apple. Then I ate all the nuts and fruit that I had packed as a snack for the drive home. I was ravenous. The stone underneath me and the sun on my face were warm and soothing. I took off my headphones and put them in the pack, looking back to the trail for any sign of my family. Nothing so far.

I stretched out on the rock. With a full belly, I felt suddenly an overwhelming wave of tiredness. "Strange woods..." I thought, as I closed my eyes, waiting for the sound of my family emerging from the forest.

I awoke suddenly, and saw that the sun was low in the sky. I was shocked to see that it was three in the afternoon. I had napped for... what? Four hours? How could that be?

I stood up, shaking off the remnants of sleep. Without

the sun shining fully on the lake, it now looked almost black, an impossibly deep lake in these strange Wisconsin woods. Where was my family? *Four hours?* I grabbed my phone to call them but saw that I had no signal.

I got scared then. Even if something had happened to one of them, they would have come to get me. Could something have happened to all of them? I began running back down the trail toward where we had separated. "Mom! Dad!" I cried out. "Luke! Where are you guys?" I felt tears coming and fought against it. I yelled, again and again. The hazy green air of the forest felt sickening. In the dimmer light of the afternoon, the colorful flowers seemed dulled. I was gasping for air, fighting rising panic. I leaned against the smooth bark of a tree, trying to calm my nerves. Why was I so dizzy?

I saw movement out of the corner of my eyes. I turned my head, slowly, looking behind me into the woods. There was something large moving through the kaleidoscope of flowers. It was dark and silent. Its yellow eyes seemed to be fixed on me. It was turning to walk towards me.

... Aren...

I turned and ran down the trail. It seemed to stretch before me for miles and miles, the wonderland of red trees and flowers on both sides now seeming like something out of a nightmare. My heart was pounding in my chest as I imagined the creature running silently down the trail behind me, getting closer and closer, its hind legs flexing as it readied to pounce...

I turned to look back and tripped, falling into the brush on the side of the path. I gagged with the cloying sweetness of the flowers. The flowers seemed almost to lean forward on their stalks, eager to press against my face. I pushed myself up to look back down the path.

Nothing. No creature. Had I imagined it? I realized dully how thirsty I was, how my head was absolutely throbbing. I blinked slowly and tried to clear my head. The dizziness had not passed.

... Aren...

I opened my eyes and the large black creature was in front of me, maybe fifteen feet away. Its yellow eyes were unblinking. Its head hung low. I could feel it emanating a deep guttural growl. I felt paralyzed, captured by its yellow eyes.

I stood unsteadily, holding one arm out. The creature took one step forward, then another. Then it tilted back its head and howled like a wolf. This broke my fear and I leapt to my feet, turning to start climbing the tree next to me. I scrambled up the trunk as quickly as I could, waiting and dreading the feeling of that creature's jaws grabbing my leg.

But it didn't, and when I reached the lower branches I looked down and I saw it watching me from the base of the tree. "GO AWAY!" I screamed. "MOM! DAD! HELP!"

The sudden exertion of running and climbing still had my heart pounding, and felt lightheaded, my vision swimming before me. I braced myself against a few branches to prevent a fall. My food must have gone bad or something, I thought dimly. Something is not right...

... Aren...

I leaned my cheek against a branch, looking down at the creature. It had its forelegs against the base of the tree, grabbing against the bark as if it were preparing to climb. I was so tired. I looked into its glowing yellow eyes, surrounded by the endless field of flowers. Surely it wouldn't be able to climb up here, right? I blinked slowly. "Mom..."

I awoke some point later. I was on my back, looking up

into the early evening sky. It took me a moment to realize I wasn't in the tree. I was wearing something over my mouth. What...?

"Esra, she's awake!"

Then my mom and dad were kneeling over me, smiling down. I felt an intense wave of relief wash over me, tears coming to my eyes. Turning my head, I saw Luke, as well as a team of paramedics and park rangers milling about the parking lot near the entrance to the trail.

I learned that we had all suffered from hallucinations, an effect brought on by some sort of plant in these strange woods. My parents had found my brother passed out on the trail. When mom left to take my brother out of the woods, my dad had succumbed to the same effect. My mom had notified the park rangers, who had been working for the last few hours to get my dad and I out of the forest. They had been calling out to me for hours.

"There was a... wolf, or something, in the woods. Did you see that? Was that real?" I asked.

The park rangers' search dog, a black Labrador, came over at that moment, nuzzling me with his snout. I gave her a big hug, pressing my face into her fur.

9

"I put a spell on you, because you're mine."
- Jay Hawkins

THE DOLLS

We arrived at dusk at the rental house in western Michigan. The house looked unremarkable: old, a single story, with tall bushes lining all sides so that you could barely see the windows of the house behind. An old wooden swing was in the front yard, and a little doll sat there. As we pulled into the driveway, I peered at the doll, which seemed to be made of cloth, with a bright red dress. Its bright blue eyes seemed to sparkle in the sun.

We would be here for five days so that we could go to my mom's family reunion before traveling back to Jordan, where we lived. My dad worked in the State Department, and my mom was an Arabic teacher at the international school that Rashid and I attended. My mom's family were Egyptian Americans who had emigrated from Egypt in the 1970s. After living for many years in the large Arab community outside Detroit, my grandparents had retired to a big house on Lake Michigan. A house that was packed with uncles, aunts, cousins, and other relatives that had traveled from all over the world for this reunion.

My dad had volunteered that we stay at a rental. My dad liked his privacy and needed a quiet place to "decompress," as he put it. My grandparents' house, on the other hand, would be a nonstop whirlwind of conversation, card games, feasts, and late nights.

We were all tired from the journey. I just wanted to take a shower and crawl into bed. Because it was July in Michigan, it wouldn't be dark until pretty late, and I was resolved to be asleep before the sun went down. One of my favorite parts of traveling was exploring new houses. Honestly, my whole family felt the same way. We always rented houses or stayed at bed and breakfasts. Who would want to stay at a hotel when you could stay in someone's house, and explore all the weirdness and surprises that were part of most people's homes? We'd been to homes with secret passages. We'd explored locked attics with found keys. We'd found secret hideouts in backyard gardens, and taken baths in the strangest bathrooms, including once in a purple clawfoot bathtub! My brother and I loved rooting out the mysteries of the homes where we stayed. My parents liked to spread out, with separate bedrooms for the kids and living areas where they could stay up, play board games, and read. My mom always looked for good bathrooms and kitchens. "They sell houses!" she'd quip.

From the outside, aside from the strange doll on the swing and the bushes practically covering the entire front of the house, this house didn't seem like anything special. Not like the castle we'd stayed in Slovenia a few months ago, or the traditional Japanese Minka we'd stayed in last year. This looked mostly like a normal, 1950s American house. While I hadn't lived in the United States since I was a baby, I had seen enough American TV to be an expert, so I thought.

I got out of the car and took a positively bone-cracking stretch. I was so stiff from the car and the airplane... it had literally been 24 hours of travel! I could feel utter exhaustion just beneath the surface of my enthusiasm to explore the new house. I walked across the lawn to sit on the swing and examine the doll closer. It was definitely old-fashioned and seemed like it had been well-loved, with some of the seams of its red plaid dress beginning to fray. It had black hair with bright blue glass eyes, though one was hanging from its socket by a thread. "Hello," I said to it, as I picked her up. I decided I would bring her inside and slipped her into the pocket of my hoodie. I was too old to play with dolls, but I still liked them.

Don't.

I jumped at the voice and looked around. Aside from my family in the driveway across the yard, there was no one around. I shook my head, convinced that my tiredness was playing tricks on me, and I walked back to the car to get my backpack.

"Look at this cool doll I found," I said to my mom as she unloaded the trunk. My dad and brother had already gone inside.

"Neat, hon," she said absentmindedly. I could tell she wasn't paying attention, but I didn't mind. We were all tired. I grabbed my backpack and suitcase and headed to the house.

"Tell your brother and dad to get out here and grab more bags! They'd better not think I'm carrying all this in myself." She called out as I crossed the threshold into the house.

Don't!

The voice buffeted me and I took a small step back. I whirled around, looking for anyone who could be speaking. Was I going crazy? It was definitely a woman's voice, and she sounded more urgent than she had a few moments before.

"Amparo! This house is so cool!" Rashid bounded down the stairs from my left. "I'm going downstairs!" I heard him thumping down the stairs deeper into the house.

The voice forgotten, I put down my bags and started exploring. I went up the stairs Rashid had just came from in search of the bedrooms. After a short staircase, there were three bedrooms side by side, and one shared bathroom. I groaned to myself. I hated sharing bathrooms.

Two of the bedrooms were pretty small with nightstands, lamps and small closets. The third, though, was awesome, and I put my bags down immediately to claim the space. Even though it was bigger than the others, it was clearly for children. It had a bunk bed, carousel wallpaper and a kid-sized dresser. On the dresser were the craziest decorations I'd ever seen: a red lamp that looked like a camping lantern with circus images on the outside, an ancient jack-in-the-box with a creepy clown picture and old metal handle, a wind-up monkey holding cymbals. I flipped the switch on the lamp, and the circus animals began to rotate, casting large red shadows on the wall. I started to wind up the jack-in-the-box and then thought better of it. The owners here obviously had a big circus theme in mind.

The circus decorations were nothing compared to the dolls. There must have been fifty dolls on the top bunk, leaving no space for someone to actually sleep. Dozens more watched down from high shelves along the walls. They were all shapes and sizes. Bunnies, cats, elephants, babies, little girls and boys. They were all old, with worn clothing, shiny faces, and glass eyes. The eyes of every single doll were sparkling crystal blue. It was the coolest doll collection I'd ever seen in my life. I couldn't wait to check them out.

Leave.

The woman's voice echoed in my head, louder and insistent. I went to find my dad and brother. I jogged back down the stairs to the entry hall, where I could hear my mom outside loudly complaining that no was helping to unload the car. I descended another short staircase and found myself in a kitchen. "Dad? Rashid?" I called, but I had no idea where they were. This house, which seemed small from the outside, was full of surprises. "We're down here," I heard my dad say, from further away than I would have thought possible in this house. I followed the voices, exiting the kitchen though a small sliding door to again descend a short staircase into an office, with a nice reclining chair and walls full of books. I was curious about the books, but then I heard Rashid call to me from down *another* set of stairs. "Amparo! Come take a look at this! You'll never believe it."

At the bottom of the stairs, I entered what I was pretty sure was a basement, even though it opened out onto a nice backyard patio. There was a hot tub! I was trying to picture the layout of the house in my head, and I couldn't piece it together - the house reminded me of the famous artist Escher and his print called *Relativity,* where stairs ran impossibly in all directions. Shelves lined the walls, but instead of books there were hundreds of antiques. Rashid and my dad were checking them out closely. "Dad, look, I'm pretty sure that's an original Babe Ruth baseball card!" Rashid said, pointing to one of the shelves.

My dad looked dumbstruck. "I think you're right. And look, there are some original-print Batman and Superman comics. I can't believe this stuff is just sitting on shelves. And they rent this place out! I don't get it."

"What kind of stuff?" I asked, walking over to the shelves.

"Amparo, take a look around, this place is chockfull of incredible antiques! There are baseball cards, original comic books, models of classic cars, vintage cameras, a model carousel, antique plates, pristine action figures. It's wild." my dad said in awe. "*Please* don't touch anything, you don't want to know how much some of this stuff probably costs."

Leave. Leave NOW.

The woman's voice was louder, more urgent. It seemed to come from everywhere. "Did you guys hear that...?" I asked.

"What?" Rashid said, inspecting the classic carousel.

"It was kind of a woman's voice?" I said, uncertainly.

"No, Amparo. I didn't hear anything," my dad said distractedly.

"Look guys, if you turn it on, the carousel starts up!" Rashid said excitedly, and sure enough the model carousel started moving. Lights turned on and as the carousel began to move, the horses moved up and down and the little figurine children riding them moved too. A small melody began to play. My dad rushed over, annoyed that his guidance had been so quickly ignored.

I stood there uneasily, wondering what to think about the voice I was hearing. And suddenly it came again.

You were warned.

The words send shivers down my spine. The woman's voice carried a certain... finality and sounded more threatening than urgent.

"Hey guys, I'm going to go upstairs and unpack. I feel so tired suddenly." I turned to head back upstairs, wondering if I'd find my way, and put my hands in my hoodie pocket. I had forgotten that the doll from the front yard was in there. I took her out. Her eyes sparkled in the dark basement just as much as they had in the sunlight. I put her on a shelf. I didn't want to carry her around after all.

I ran upstairs, twisting and turning to get there, and found mom in the kitchen. "Hey mom, what's for dinner?" I asked.

I could see that that was probably the worst thing I could have said to her. She turned away from me, waving her arm. "No idea, Amparo! We just got here. I've been unloading the car. Got any ideas?"

"Maybe I can just order pizza? I'll find a place on my phone." I sat on a stool by the kitchen counter.

"Yes, that would be great. Thank you. Sorry I snapped, I'm just exhausted," my mom said. "I'm going to go upstairs and lie down, but here's $40 for the pizza. Wake me up when it gets here." She yawned and walked away.

After I ordered the pizza, I went to the fridge to see if there was anything to drink. In my experience, sometimes rental hosts left soda or wine or something for guests. Sure enough, there were a few cokes, and I grabbed one and began opening up the cabinets looking for glasses. I froze. Each cabinet had an antique doll on the shelves, sitting among the glasses and dishes. The one next to the coffee mugs was probably the creepiest doll I'd ever seen in my life. Its clothes were tattered and faded, though they were green and seemed almost like soldier fatigues. Its ceramic skin was cracked and dirty, though its mouth was bright red. Its head lolled sideways, and its blue eyes almost seemed to glitter with malice. What bothered me most of all was the rope loosely tied around its neck like a noose. I slowly reached out and touched it, just to double check it was solid.

I loved dolls, but I had never seen such an unsettling

creation. Who in their right mind would put dolls in kitchen cabinets? Who in the world would put a noose around the neck of such a doll? I thought maybe one of the cleaners was playing a joke on the guests. Probably the hosts didn't even know.

I quickly grabbed a glass and soda and went up to my bedroom. I was having second thoughts on picking this room. I loved dolls, but the whole house was giving me the creeps. The voice, the creepy doll, the weird circus décor... even the surreal layout of the house, which normally I would have found exciting, was putting me on edge. I grabbed my suitcase and started pulling it to the next room. If I went quick, I could nab it before Rashid.

As I pulled it into the hallway, Rashid wandered out of the other bedroom yawning. "Hey sis! Is the pizza ordered? What did you get?"

I dragged my bag back into the room. I guess I was stuck. I unpacked quickly under the watchful gaze of a hundred blue glass eyes. I practically ran to the front door when the pizza delivery gal rang the doorbell. After pizza, the jetlag hit and we all went to bed. I tried to read in the light of the red circus lamp, but soon fell asleep.

Around midnight, I woke up having to pee. I went across the hall to the bathroom, navigating the room in the dark to the toilet. The house was black and silent around me. I sat there, groggily looking at the shower curtain pulled across the bathtub in front of me while I finished.

Music began to play. My eyes widened, the sleepiness suddenly driven from my body. Circus music, soft and tinny, echoed on the tiles of the bathroom. In the absolute silence of the house it sounded enormous, like it was coming from everywhere. But as I listened, goosebumps spreading on my arms, I knew: it was coming from the bathtub.

My hand shook as I reached forward to grab the shower curtain. Over and over again the circus music repeated the same few notes. I yanked the curtain to the side, and as I did the music stopped.

In the basin of the tub was the toy carousel from the basement. The same one Rashid had wound up that night, I was sure of it. Its small mechanical horses were still inching around their cycle, slowing down as the carousel ended its tune.

I stood, staring at the toy. Rashid, I thought with a sudden conviction. He *had* to be the one that put it here. I didn't know how he had set it to go off in the middle of the night, but it seemed like the kind of prank he'd do. I vowed to get him back the next day.

The next morning, we were in a rush to get ready and get to the lake house for the family reunion. We felt much better after a night of sleep. I went to the bathroom to get the carousel and confront my brother, though it was gone. No doubt he had already moved it. Rashid was running behind, as usual, searching the house frantically for his bathing suit. How does one lose a bathing suit in less than a day from unpacking? I had no idea, but it was annoying the rest of us. As we waited impatiently by the front door, Rashid finally came downstairs holding his bathing suit in one hand. In the other hand, I saw he was holding the doll with the red dress that I had found outside yesterday. The one I had left in the basement. For some reason seeing it again, one eye hanging on its cheek, gave me a feeling of unease.

"Very funny Amparo," Rashid said with an angry look.

He knew mom and dad were getting annoyed with him. "You buried my suit in the toy basket in your closet? With this ugly thing? Real nice."

I was speechless. "I... well at least I didn't freak you out in the middle of the night, Rashid."

"What? What are you.." Rashid responded before my mom intervened. "Okay. Can we go? Or do you want to explain to the family that we were late because you two were too busy messing with each other?" My mom had a way of asking questions that weren't really questions. We had all learned that the best strategy was to stay quiet. Rashid and I glared at each other as we got in the car and left.

We had a great first day at the reunion. I loved seeing my cousins especially, who I hadn't seen in ages and who seemed a lot more interesting than I remembered. We shared stories, swam in the lake, and ate an unbelievable amount. My grandparents knew how to throw a family party, and it was a wonderful day. The jetlag, food, and a day in the sun had us all exhausted as we got back to the rental in the late evening.

The day had been so lovely that it wasn't until we entered the house that my unease came back in a rush. I was not looking forward to seeing the dolls again. I resolved to turn all the dolls around to face the walls before going to bed. I no longer thought the dolls were cute. They were creepy, and I didn't want them and their blue glass eyes staring at me while I slept.

As I was turning the dolls around one by one, my mom called to me from the kitchen. I came downstairs, where she was drying dishes and putting them back on the shelves. "Amparo, did you move the dolls?" The shelves, which that morning during breakfast still had been adorned with antique dolls, now only held dishes and glasses.

"No..." I thought of Rashid again and wondered for a second whether this was another prank. But when would he have done it? We were gone all day...

"Maybe the property managers came by and collected them. Anyway, can you help me put these dishes away?"

I went back upstairs, listening to Rashid singing terribly in the shower. I walked into my room. "Oh, no no no no no no..." I murmured to myself. All the dolls were again with their backs to the walls. Their blue eyes sparkled.

When Rashid came out of the bathroom, he found me in a blanket on the floor of his room. I was done with the circus horror show. I had slept on the floor during our travels before and had no problem doing it again.

"Uh, Amparo, what are you doing?"

"I'm sleeping here tonight. Don't snore."

"Ughh..." He groaned, but thankfully did not put up a fight. We were too tired. In minutes we were asleep.

At midnight, like clockwork, I was up again to pee. I was relieved to see that the shower curtain was left open, and the bathtub was empty. I listened to the house, dreading the sound of circus music, but it remained silent. I quietly started to return to Rashid's room.

In the hall I saw that the door to my bedroom was cracked open. Shifting red light shone through the crack. I knew that red light. Knowing that I was making a mistake, I slowly pushed open the door.

The red lantern on the nightstand was on, the animals rotating soundlessly. The enormous shadows of giraffes and elephants were cast against the wall, their shape constantly changing as they moved across the furniture of the room. My focus, however, was not on the shadows. I stared in horror at the bed I had slept in the previous night. All of the dolls from the room were on the bed, covering every inch. Dozens and dozens of dolls, blue eyes catching the light of the lantern. The shelves above were empty, the bunkbed empty. The doll in the red dress, I saw, sat closest to the door. One of its arms was up, hand bent. Beckoning me to enter.

On the nightstand, the wind-up monkey crashed his cymbals together. I shrieked and fled.

I ran to my parents' room in a panic. "Mom, dad, please, I'm sorry, wake up." My dad started and sat up, bleary-eyed, and turned on his side lamp. "Amparo... calm down... what is it...?" Rashid wandered into the room behind me rubbing his eyes.

I began to speak but saw that mom was not in the bed. Her covers were thrown back. On her pillow was a small rope noose. "Dad..." I pointed a shaking hand.

At that moment we heard my mom cry out, a distant sound, from somewhere in the bowels of the house.

We ran downstairs. The kitchen was empty, the living room empty. We continued further down. The office was empty. From the unlit staircase to the basement, we heard the soft sound of circus music. We ran downstairs and threw on the lights.

Mom was laying on the floor of the basement. Her eyes were wide but cloudy and unseeing, as if she were sleepwalking. She was in the center of a circle of dolls, dozens of dolls. The largest doll in its green outfit I recognized from the kitchen. Its cracked ceramic face was turned toward us, and I gasped when I saw that a pair of scissors lay next to its small hands.

My dad ran to mom and gathered her in his arms. "Honey, honey, are you okay? Wake up." He and I saw at the same time

that mom's ponytail had been cut off, its hair strewn around the circle of dolls. "Dad, we need to leave this house," I said urgently. The carousel on the shelf nearby was continuing to play its tune, though it seemed to be growing louder.

He looked at me and nodded. "I... I think you're right. We'll go to the lake house."

We gathered our things and were on the road in minutes. As soon as we were out of the house, mom started to wake up, and by the time we were out of the neighborhood she was back to normal.

We were about halfway to the lake house when my dad stopped for gas. I got out to stretch my legs and grab my tablet from the trunk. I opened the trunk and screamed. On top of my luggage was the doll in the red dress, staring at me with her one crystal blue eye, the other dangled by a thread. Most horribly of all, it had a sweeping red stitch of a smile across its face where none had been before.

I told you.

10

"I just can't wake from these scary dreams."
-Ozzy Osbourne

SCREAMCATCHER

Freya's green eyes twinkled when she saw the dream catcher hanging in the basement window. Light from the basement window filtered through the strands of the dream catcher. She could hear faint sounds from the busy Brooklyn Street beyond the glass. Far away, she heard her mom talking to the creepy old woman that ran this antique shop, negotiating prices or asking about the background of an old vase, or something.

She had been wandering this antique shop for at least an hour. It was the third that day, and she was getting thoroughly sick of trying to be interested in old junk. This shop seemed to specialize in American antiques, maybe especially from the Southwest and Native American cultures. She had eventually found herself in the basement. Motes of dust floated in the air as she walked through rows and rows of old photos of unsmiling Native American families, pottery, and artwork. She absentmindedly brushed away a spiderweb as she moved into a small clearing at the far end of the basement. And there she found the dream catcher.

The clearing was surrounded by a collection of beautiful dream catchers and antique music boxes. She sat in a children's rocking chair and admired the details of the dream catchers. Each had colored stones woven into the threads, creating a kaleidoscope of light that danced on the shelves around the clearing. One dream catcher in particular caught her eye. It was the only one in a glass case. She stood to look more closely at it, admiring its red, ruby-like stones and the blue feathers that hung from the bottom. The stones seemed almost bottomless with dull red light. The black latticework was impossibly intricate, she thought. The threads looked finer than silk, and Freya was struck with an overwhelming urge to touch those threads, to look more deeply into the red stones. Her hands found the glass case locked, and without thinking she lifted a nearby music box and brought it down on the lock, breaking it off. She listened to see if anyone upstairs had heard the noise. When no one came, she opened the cabinet and carefully removed the dream catcher.

A breeze blew softly through the basement then, and her curly blond hair blew with it. She felt cold, and the light from the street window grew dim. She turned and saw that all the music boxes were open, each playing strange music. The hairs on her neck stood up. She moved to leave but, in a sudden impulse, she took the dream catcher, putting it in her backpack before running upstairs. Away from the unsettling twirl of feathers and colored stones and the discordant tunes of the music boxes. She had never stolen anything before that day, and as time would tell, she never would again.

"Please, tell me what happened."

"Well, I guess the start was about a week ago. Just a little over a week ago, actually... around the time we got back from New York. Freya has been having just awful night terrors. I know this happens with some kids, so I've tried to not make a big deal out of it, but they really have been terrible. None of us can sleep."

"Yes, night terrors are fairly common with kids Freya's age. I understand how scary they can be. But don't worry, they will go away as she gets older."

"Doctor, I get it, I really do, but... I can't describe how frightening this has been for us. I've read a lot over the last week about night terrors, and this seems worse."

"Mary, why don't you tell me the whole story. From the beginning."

"Well, we got back from New York City last week. Last Sunday. It was our first big post-pandemic trip, so we went a little overboard with shopping, exploring the boroughs, going to a Broadway show, visiting the Statue of Liberty, all that kind of stuff. Basically living the big city life, big change of pace from the small town lifestyle around here. We did a lot of antiquing, actually, which I was really missing during the pandemic. It was a magical trip. Seems like years ago now... the night terrors started when we got back.

"Freya usually tells us she can't remember her dreams but beginning last Sunday night, when she woke up in the morning she told us in great detail a terrible dream. About a man in our house, with a knife, who was hunting our dog, Rover. This man—and I'll never forget how she described it—she said he approached her, in the dream, asking where Rover was. His eyes were bloody red orbs in his face, and his face was like a nest of thin black snakes, all twisting and turning over themselves. He had this gaping mouth filled with teeth like razor blades. That's how she described it, I still can't believe my little girl was telling me these things. She really doesn't ever remember her dreams but she told us this one, and she was shaking at the breakfast table like she was freezing cold. I swear, even Rover seemed scared from Freya's dream, he was hiding under the bed almost the whole day."

"That poor girl, that sounds just terrible. Did something happen in New York? Something that bothered her?"

"No, we had an amazing trip. Like I said, it was magical. But it all disappeared quickly. After that first night, Freya has become afraid to sleep at night. She's even fallen asleep in school a couple of times, which never happens and has had her teachers calling us.

"It's not the same every night. Sometimes it's like that first night, when she describes some awful nightmare. Other times she has woken up screaming bloody murder in the middle of the night, talking about bloody eyes and knives and people breaking in to the house. Black snakes... Such violent dreams. Stuff that she's never heard us talking about, let alone seen on TV.

"So I'm sure you can imagine, the rest of us haven't been sleeping much either. We began taking shifts after the first couple days. One of us would sit in her room in the rocker and watch over her and try to let the rest of the family get some actual rest."

"Does she ever sleepwalk?"

"Funny you should ask... This is what convinced us to talk to a psychiatrist. So a couple nights ago, I was in the rocker in her room. I eventually fell asleep. Actually had a nightmare myself, I guess Freya's stories were starting to get to me. Anyway, I woke up in the middle of the night to this awful pounding sound coming from downstairs. I thought I was still dreaming, but my husband came into the room, and then I saw that Freya wasn't in her bed. We followed the sound down to the kitchen, and we found Freya sitting at our kitchen table, just pounding a hammer into the table. She was doing it hard enough that she had actually started to splinter the wood. Can you imagine? A little eight-year-old girl in her PJs, alone in the dark kitchen, hammering the table over and over and over... Rover was there too, I remember that vividly, he was growling the whole time. It took us a few minutes to wake her up. Her dream, my god, she told us how she had been dreaming about that bloodred-eyes person, or thing, and it was chasing her and her brother through the house. She was defending herself with the hammer. Her arms and legs were all bruised up, I guess from banging around in the dark in the house while she was sleepwalking.

"What do we do, doctor? I am out of ideas."

"...I... sorry, I'm a little bit at a loss for words. I've never heard of night terrors like that. I can't imagine what your family is going through. How is your son handling this? Is he having nightmares too, or is it only Freya?"

"He's upset because Freya is upset, but he's eighteen months old. His sleep hasn't really changed. He sleeps like the dead."

"Look, I'm not sure what's happening with your daughter. I will need to see her and talk to her. A sleep study at the hospital might be a good idea, but until we can schedule those appointments, I'd like to prescribe a sedative. It is perfectly safe, I assure you, and the main thing is that you will all be able to get a good night's sleep. When can you bring her in, and when will you be available to conduct a sleep study?"

"We are ready as soon as you are."

"Hi Freya. I'm Dr. Wills, but you can call me Sue if you want to. It's very nice to meet you."

"Hi."

"I've been talking to your mom a bit about some of the bad dreams you've been having. How are you doing today? Have you been getting some sleep?"

"No. Not really."

"I'm so sorry to hear that. It's not fun to have nightmares. Can you tell me about them?"

"I don't want to. I want the bad people to stay away."

"I... understand. Do you mind if your mother tells me about the last couple of nights?"

"So, the sedative did not seem to help at all. Freya has had two more terrible nights of sleep since I last saw you. Last night, Robert and I were woken up by our dog barking furiously downstairs, at the back door. We went to check on him and found the door was wide open. Freya was standing out in the yard. She was standing under a tree, punching it and clawing it with all of her might. Robert got a black eye when he tried to pull her away. I mean, look at her hands, doctor. We spent an hour bandaging her hands last night."

"And... what did Freya say, when she woke up?"

"It was like before. She was fighting with a red-eyed monster that seemed to made of black ropes or snakes or something. He was trying to kill her, or eat her, and she was defending herself. And... not only that, but she has started muttering to herself and even thrashing as soon as she falls asleep. It's like she's immediately dreaming these terrible dreams."

"Freya, I would like to increase the sedative, a little bit, and we're going to do a brain scan. I know that sounds scary but it is very quick and easy, you don't feel anything at all. Would that be ok?"

"Sure."

"What happened? You sounded so anxious on the phone."

"The nightmares have spread. We're all dreaming it now, doctor."

"Tell me."

"The night after we saw you, we gave her a higher dose of the sedative, as you had advised. She fell asleep very fast, although like I said, she started moaning and muttering to herself within minutes. Honestly, we all fell asleep pretty fast after she did, we've been so exhausted.

"I had such a vivid dream. You can probably guess what it was about, but I will tell you anyway. I was in our house, though it felt different. Darker. The halls were narrower, the ceiling was higher. The air felt *thick*, in some strange way. I heard a voice in the house, coming from everywhere it seemed. It was talking to me, telling me what it was going to do. When it found me. I knew immediately whose voice it was, even before it came up the stairs. It was just as Freya had described. It was tall and black, with bloody marbles for eyes and a mouth that just hung open filled with teeth like glass. Its face and body, everything, was a coiling and twisting mound of black cords or ropes. It was the most horrible thing. It came into my bedroom. It was still talking the whole time."

"My god Mary. Everyone is having these dreams?"

"Yes. I don't know what would have happened next because I woke up from yelling in the house. I went downstairs and found Robert in the living room. He had been yelling for me. He had woken up and found himself carving shapes and symbols into the floor of our living room with a kitchen knife. He had been doing that *while he was asleep.* And that's not even the worst. We heard crying outside, and it was our baby boy Luke by the swimming pool. He was soaking wet, as if he fell into the pool, and Rover was there soaking wet too, I have to assume the dog pulled him out of the pool. Saved his life.

"Doctor, we feel like we're losing our minds. I don't know what we can do. We can't go to sleep. What will happen next time we fall asleep?"

I pull into the driveway. I sit in the car for several minutes, looking at the front door. I wonder if we should leave, maybe sleep at a hotel. Then I see Freya in the window, and get out and go to her.

Freya is withdrawn and scared. I sit with her, holding hands and leaning on one another. I could feel her trembling slightly.

"Mom... I have to show you something," Freya says. She takes my hand and leads me to her bedroom.

In her picture perfect kids room with her pink panda bedspread, her half a dozen stuff animals and her bookshelf overflowing with kids books, I sit down in the bean bag chair at the foot of her bed and drag her into my lap. "What did you want to show me," I ask Freya.

She points then at the window, and that's when I notice it. In the window above her bed, there's a dream catcher. It is striking - in the light of the morning the red stones in its black threads glow like small balls of fire.

"Where did you get that, honey?" I ask.

Suddenly, Freya begins to cry. "I *stole* it. When we went to New York," she sobs. Through her tears, she explains how she took it from the antique store in Brooklyn. "I didn't want to take it! I couldn't help it. It forced me to take it."

She sniffled. "I think... I think it's giving us the nightmares."

"Honey, I understand you feel badly about taking the dream catcher. Stealing is wrong. But a little piece of string and feathers is not giving us nightmares. That's a fairytale." I feel like I need to be more stern about her theft, but I draw her closer for a hug instead.

"Still, we need to contact the store and arrange to send it back," I say, "and, you need to tell your dad. He's not going to be happy, but honesty will make you feel better. Could even help you sleep." I give her a kiss on the forehead. "I don't know what is causing these nightmares, honey, but we will figure it out. This too will pass."

While Robert sternly talks to Freya about how stealing is wrong, I dig around my purse to find the card the antique shop. I find it and call, putting the phone on speaker. Freya needed to be part of this conversation and apologize, and then we could put this behind us.

The antique shop owner picks up on the third ring, and I tell her who I am. She sounds annoyed by the call, like she was busy with something else. But, as soon as I tell her that my daughter needed to speak with her, and as soon as she hears my daughter's scared voice, she grows silent. Attentive.

Freya tells her everything. About how she broke into the locked cabinet and took the dream catcher. Details that she hadn't told me, about music boxes that started to play on their own. She starts to talk about the nightmares, as well, and I almost intervene to stop her, but for some reason it seems to be part of the same story. She tells much more than I would have shared, but it feels right. Somehow.

When Freya is done, the woman doesn't say anything for a long time. Finally, I clear my voice and ask if she is still on the line. In a quiet voice, she responds, and the words shake me to my core.

"You have great evil in your home now." She says slowly. "You must bring that dream catcher back at once. Do not sleep until you do. It will kill your family. I am surprised it hasn't taken Freya already." Anger grew in her voice. Robert and I look at each other with raised eyebrows. "She can't be serious?" I mouth the words.

"I know you don't believe me." she says. Freya protests, and the woman continued, "I know *you* do, child. But your parents don't. You must come at once. Your lives depend on this! I will wait at the store for you." And with that, she ends the call.

We sit in silence for a moment, and then Robert says, "There is no way we can get to Brooklyn today. It's already six. Can you imagine the traffic? It will take six hours to get there. And honestly, honey, I will fall asleep on the road. I am so exhausted." He is adamant. "Do we really believe what she's saying? I fully agree that Freya needs to return the dream catcher, but I was thinking we could mail it..."

"But Dad! You heard her! We have to go!" Freya has tears in her eyes.

"Freya... I have to agree with your dad. It is just too late for us to go to New York right now. *But...* we will go tomorrow morning, first thing. Ok? It would be too dangerous for us to drive at night, as tired as we are." Robert is looking at me, eyebrows raised at my assertion that we will go to New York in the morning. Freya, on the other hand, looks away. The deep fear in her eyes hits me like a punch, and I wonder, for a moment, if we have made the wrong choice.

Mary.

I wake up.

The room is the blackest black. The drapes on the windows, which I had left open last night to allow in some moonlight, are drawn. I can make out the slightest outline of the doorframe leading into the hall. I reach out to feel the bed next to me, searching for Robert, but the sheets are empty and cool.

Mary. I told you I would find you.

I hear the voice, a guttural deep sound that seems to come from the walls, the bed, the moon, from everywhere. I know exactly what is making the sound, and my eyes go wide in horror. I must still be asleep, I thought. This is only a dream, and dreams cannot hurt you. They *cannot.*

You are wrong, Mary. Dreams can be very, very painful.

Two bloodred orbs open in the doorway. Floating in the darkness. The deep black starts to come together around those bloodred eyes, into a hundred thousand writhing black threads. They grow larger as the thing enters the room. Below them, I know there is a deeper darkness filled with endless teeth.

I grab the lamp next to me and throw it across the room. It

shatters on the creature, but it does not slow. It moves to stand beside the bed.

Give me your fears.

Its black tendril arms reach down and I think for a moment of the dream catcher. I imagine it in Freya's window, spinning softly even without a breeze, its red stones growing brighter and fatter as they drank in the horrors in the house. I could feel the ice-cold tendrils of the thing's arms...

"NO! Mom! Dad!"

I gasp and wake up.

Robert is above me, his eyes cloudy. One hand presses down on me, pinning me to the bed. In the other, a kitchen knife is held high. The moonlight catches on its point.

"Dad!"

Freya shouts from the doorway, and as she does Rover bounds on to the bed and into Robert, causing him to stumble backwards and drop the knife. I see he has shards of our bedside lamp stuck in the folds of his nightshirt. I guess I really did throw it, I think dizzily.

Robert shakes his head, and I can see he is himself again. "Mary... what...?"

We leave within the hour back to New York. It is the middle of the night, but we could not stay there a minute longer. Robert and I don't talk much on the drive. We aren't sure what was happening, but we both felt with a conviction that Freya and the old woman were right. I grabbed the dream catcher just before we left, and I admitted to myself that I had been terrified for a moment that touching the dream catcher would cause... something... to happen. But nothing did, and I had thrown it in the trunk.

We arrive at the antique shop as the sun was coming up.

We find the door to the shop locked. "Are you kidding me," Robert mutters as he rings the door again and again.

Finally, we hear the rustling of keys on the other side. The great oak door creaks open, and the shop owner stands on the other side. She seems even older than she did when we were there two weeks ago. Her withered face was pinched from years of wrinkles closing in on themselves. Her beady black eyes, deep within their sockets, gives each of us a piercing look, and she waves us soundlessly inside.

She leads us to her study on the first floor, through rows and rows of antiques. The musty air is dense in her office, and we sit together on an old brown leather couch by the window. She sits slowly in a red velvet armchair in front of us. As she takes a long sip of tea, I realize she has not yet spoken since we entered the shop.

"The dream catcher came into my life when I was 22." She begins slowly. "I had just moved to New York with my husband. We had decided to start an antique collection after an estate sale upstate. She had been a hoarder, though they didn't call it that in those days. She was a "collector" but the reality was that when she died, they sold off her estate in batches, as it was too much to parcel out piece by piece. It was fortuitous for us, just starting out. And we enjoyed going through the forty boxes we received piece by piece, appraising and marking each piece for our newly set up store space." She clears her throat.

"One of the last boxes had a medium sized black leather box with multiple locking mechanisms. We worked on those locks for days, it was like a game. We were very foolish... but we finally got it open.

"The box was lined with lead, but we didn't think anything

of it. We were too distracted by the dream catcher, which is truly beautiful. And, as I imagine the young lady knows," she says, winking at Freya, "the dream catcher can have a certain... influence over you. We were bewitched, plain and simple."

She sighs and is silent for a minute. "The nightmares began that night. Within a week, my brother in law had killed himself. Jumped off a roof. My new husband tried to kill me with a knife, and he later stabbed himself to death." She pauses to dab her eyes.

"I couldn't believe it. My world was shattered, months after I had been happily married. I did not yet understand the cause of my distress, and I kept having terrible nightmares. Maybe two weeks after opening the box, I took the dream catcher to a jeweler to have it appraised. I left it with him, and that night had the first night of peaceful sleep in weeks. His nightmares began, though, and within days he and his wife were dead.

"After I heard what happened, I understood. I got the box and the dream catcher back and kept it locked for years. I didn't know what to do with it, in truth, I just wanted to make sure it never fell into another person's hands. I kept up my dead husband's dream and continued building our antique shop. Many, many years ago, the case was damaged in a fire, and I had a special lead-lined glass case made to hold it. The dream catcher of course wasn't damaged in the fire... I'm not sure anything could truly destroy it. Oh, the nightmares I had during those days, waiting for the new case to be made, I wouldn't wish them on anyone...

"The dream catcher, as best I can tell, is a nightmare catcher. Instead of catching and bringing good dreams to its owners, it brings the most horrific and violent nightmares. It has a kind of evil intelligence or spirit inside of it."

Freya pulls the nightmare catcher from her backpack then, and the withered old woman recoils as if struck.

"The evil in this thing has been contained for decades and has now had another taste of freedom. A taste of fear, I suppose, which is what it really wants. We must lock it back in the cabinet, and perhaps I shall bury it this time." She gingerly takes the nightmare catcher, and we walk down to the basement and to the old display cabinet. The woman carefully places it back within on a hook and locks the cabinet with new locks.

Immediately, a deep wave of relief washes over me. I can see the same on the faces of Robert and Freya as well.

That night, back in our home, we sleep peacefully. In the antique shop, the nightmare catcher twists and turns in its case, its red stones glowing dully. And upstairs, the old woman cries out in her sleep.

ABOUT THE AUTHORS

Kelley Laird & Matt Wills

With two creative kids and two enthusiastic dogs, they are never happier than when they are frightening their kids with creepy tales. They love the outdoors and scary stories around the campfire. When they aren't being harassed by their children to tell them more stories or play D&D in Maryland, they enjoy traveling, board gaming, and cooking together. Find Kelley on Facebook at Kelley E Laird.

ABOUT THE ILLUSTRATORS

Emma Mackela

Is a freelance artist and tattooist working out of Kalamazoo, Michigan. Her portfolio received a National Silver Medal by Scholastics Awards in the USA, and she works for Run for Cover Records to do band merchandizing. She is passionate about oil and acrylic art, spending time with her partner and three lizards. Find her on Instagram at @emmamackela or reach out to emmacmackela@gmail.com

Miha Brumec

An illustrator and digital artist from tiny Slovenia. He loves world mythologies and history and brings these perspectives to his art. He has loved the fantasy since reading *The Hobbit* as a kid, still enjoys playing RPGs and fantasy games of all types. Find him on Instagram at @mihabrumecart

Made in the USA
Monee, IL
02 November 2024

69176175R00089